A Fairy Match in the Mushroom Patch

Also by Amanda M. Thrasher

The Mischief Series
Book 1 • *Mischief in the Mushroom Patch*
Book 3 • *A Spider Web Scramble in the Mushroom Patch*
(Coming Soon)

The Ghost of Whispering Willow

A Fairy Match in the Mushroom Patch

Amanda M. Thrasher

RISING PHOENIX PRESS

Published 2013 by Progressive Rising Phoenix Press.
www.progressiverisingphoenix.com

ISBN: 0988856816
ISBN-13: 978-0-9888568-1-3

Printed in the U.S.A.
3rd Printing

Edited by Anne Dunigan

DEDICATION

This book is dedicated to a precious girl I never knew.
Though I never met her, those that knew
her loved her dearly.
She would have adored little Pearle,
I am certain of it!

CONTENTS

1	Fairies at Play	1
2	Tricks in the Class-Schroom	15
3	Flight 101	31
4	The Race is On	45
5	Rolled Fern Seed	63
6	Nonstop Rain	75
7	Fairy Dust Demonstration	88
8	Disaster at Hand	103
9	Team Work	114
10	Kick-a-Berry	128
11	The Match	137

1 • FAIRIES AT PLAY

Laying on a rock in the middle of the brook, Lilly, sunned herself, as her friends danced and giggled around her. The sun felt wonderful as it tickled the tips of her delicate wings and she felt content. Her mind wandered, and she was startled when Boris called out her name.

"Lilly you're it! It's your turn!" Boris yelled playfully as he leapt from lily pad to lily pad. "We know you're awake," he giggled. "Let's play, Lilly, while we have time. *Come on*!"

Lilly sat up just in time to watch Boris land clumsily on a lily pad that didn't look as if it could quite hold his weight! *This does not look good,* Lilly thought, trying hard not to giggle as she watched Boris leap to another lily pad that was directly in front of him. Lilly leapt to her feet, hoping to warn him. She yelled at the top of her tiny voice, "Boris, the pad, it's . . . " But it was too late, and she could tell by the look on poor Boris's face that he knew all too well what was about to happen.

Boris's arms and legs waved in the air and his wings flailed frantically, though they did not manage to help him keep his balance. Boris went head first into the brook – fully clothed at that!

It was Ivy who first ran to Boris's aid. She tried to help him, but she was simply too small. Lilly rushed to her side to assist, but after taking one look at Boris, she was no help at all. Though she was trying hard not to, Lilly's giggling had turned to full-fledged laughter at the very sight of her dear friend, Boris, sitting in the middle of the brook all covered in moss. She tried to bite her little lip as she tugged Ivy, who was trying to pull Boris out of the water. She even tried to think of how she would feel if she were the one smack in the middle of the deepest part of the brook and covered in moss, but the harder she tried to stop laughing, the worse her laughter became. She felt terrible; guilty in fact, because she couldn't stop no matter how hard she tried. Her cheeks became flushed, and she couldn't talk.

Her big, bright, blue eyes filled with tears, but to Boris's dismay, they were tears of laughter. Finally, Lilly composed herself long enough to say, "Oh, Boris." But that was it; that was all she could manage at the moment. "Oh Boris!" Then she started laughing all over again.

Boris's clothes, naturally soaked through, were covered in nasty green moss, as was his hair. His face scrunched up in disgust. The water he had accidently swallowed tasted awful at best and Lilly could see Boris was trying desperately to get rid of the taste from his mouth. She could tell he was having absolutely no luck at all, since he kept spluttering and spitting out the water. Each time Boris tried to stand up he slipped, which only made the laughter he heard coming from the bank worse. Adding insult to injury, Ivy had started to giggle, too.

Lilly tried to speak to Boris again, "Oh Boris, I'm so sorry," she said. "I don't mean to laugh, I really don't, but you just look, well, you just look awful!"

She quickly clasped her tiny little hands over her mouth, hardly believing the words had actually slipped out of her mouth at all. She was quite shocked, really. She knew that wasn't a very nice thing to say, especially to her friend, Boris, of all fairlings. She tried to apologize again, though she was sure she didn't sound convincing at all.

"Oh Boris, I'm so sorry. I am." She took a deep breath. "I'm not really laughing because you fell in the brook," she said. Boris didn't look like he believed her. "I'm laughing because well, you look – oh my goodness – I'm just sorry!" she managed, suddenly feeling ashamed she had been laughing at all!

Boris tried to stand up again. He took one step forward and slipped due to the slippery mud beneath him, landing on his rear end again! Once again he sat in the water, covered in moss, with

a look of despair etched on his face. He stared up at his friends.

"Any suggestions?" he asked. "Any at all?"

"Grab my hand, Boris," Lilly said, extending her hand. "Ivy will grab me and together we will pull you out. Come on!" She was certain they could manage this task.

Boris reached for Lilly's hand. Ivy held onto Lilly with all of her might, though her feet were slipping in the soggy mud on the bank of the brook, Ivy held firm. Lilly leaned way over the brook, her fingertips touching the tips of Boris's fingers. *A little closer*, she thought as she leaned toward Boris, *just a little closer.*

"Almost Lilly, almost," said Boris.

Lilly knew she was not quite close enough and glanced at Ivy, who nodded her head. It was a sure sign Ivy was holding onto Lilly tightly. Lilly leaned toward Boris a little more. Boris managed to grab her hand. Together, Ivy and Lilly pulled Boris to his feet. However, as soon as he started to move forward, he slipped to the left, and then slipped to the right. Boris could not get his footing despite how hard he tried. The mud beneath him was sticky and slick, and the boulders scattered throughout were dangerous. If the little fairlings were not careful, Boris could slip and hit his head. Try as they may, Ivy and Lilly were simply not strong enough to pull Boris out of the babbling brook. Boris suddenly had the oddest look on his face, as if something had just occurred to him. It had – Jack!

"Hang on," Boris said with a grin, "we just need one more. Where's Jack?"

Jack was nowhere in sight. He had made a mad dash toward the woods right after he yelled, "Hide and go find a fairling . . . Lilly's it!" The little fairlings looked around, but hey could see no sign of him. Hide and go find a fairling was one of Jack's favorite games, and he was very good at it. It was likely they wouldn't find Jack for a while, unless he was watching them and came out on his own. Lilly stepped back onto the bank with Ivy. She cupped her tiny hands to her mouth and proceeded to yell at the top of her voice.

"Jack!" she cried, "Jack we need you, we need your help. Come on out, game over and you win!"

There was no answer. They peered all around them, but there was still no sign of Jack. Once again Lilly cupped her hands to her mouth as did Ivy, and together they yelled his name. Still Jack did not come out.

"It looks like it's you and me, Lilly," Ivy said trying her best not to giggle at poor Boris. Lilly, after all, had done a fabulous job demonstrating her lack of self-control regarding this delicate, slightly embarrassing situation that their dear friend Boris found himself in. Lilly extended her little arm, as she firmly planted her feet on the bank. She waited to feel the tiny arms of Ivy wrapped securely around her waist before she leaned closer toward Boris.

"Here we go Boris, we'll try again," Lilly said softly. "Grab my arm and Ivy and I will pull you out of the brook and onto the bank."

Lilly planted her feet on the slippery bank, and once

again Ivy dug in her heels and leaned as far back as she could, hoping to stabilize Lilly.

"Are you ready Boris, we're ready . . . are you?" Lilly asked softly as she extended her hand toward him. Her hands were shaking, as were her knees, since she, too, was slipping in the mud. Boris, had a very odd look on his little round face. Lilly was trying very hard to differentiate the new look Boris was suddenly wearing, but she couldn't. Boris extended his plump little hand toward Lilly and nodded his head.

"*Really*," Boris said for no particular reason, which Lilly found rather bizarre, and so did Ivy given the circumstances.

"Yes, really Boris. Grab my hand. We'll pull you out in no time at all!" Lilly said, although she was starting to think Boris had been in the brook too long, and that the water had made more than his britches soggy.

"Really," Boris said yet again, and this time Ivy thought he sounded and looked rather strange. With a puzzled look on her face, Ivy tightened her grip around Lilly's waist and buckled down. Then, in unison, Lilly and Ivy shouted, "Yes, Boris, really!"

"Grab my hand," Lilly repeated again, glancing at Ivy

with raised brows. She muttered a quiet *tut* under her breath, shook her head and whispered, "We have to get him out of there."

Boris reached out and grabbed Lilly's hand, "Okay then one more time," he said. "On the count of three?"

Lilly and Ivy nodded – together agreeing that three was a great number to pull on. They started the countdown. "One, two, three," they said together. On the third count Ivy pulled Lilly, Lilly pulled Boris, and Boris pulled both of them as hard as he possibly could. A final yank of Lilly's hand and Ivy lost her balance as her feet slipped from underneath her. Poor Lilly ended up smack in the middle of the brook, next to Boris. Suddenly there was another great big splash, and a tiny scream, followed by two laughing fairlings, one on the bank and one in the brook. Two very upset little fairies sat in the brook, one landed on top of Boris, and one right next to him. All three fairlings were covered in slime, a combination of wet mud, moss, and peat.

"Jack!" cried Lilly, "I should have known . . . but didn't… but I should have known!" she yelled as best she could while spitting moss out of her mouth. "Oh Jack, and you… Boris!"

"Boris," sobbed Ivy, "WHY ON EARTH DID YOU DO THAT?" and then she looked up. "Jack!" she cried, "Why did YOU do that?"

It was Boris that couldn't answer this time, for he was laughing so hard at precious little Lilly. Her golden curls gone, her beautifully sunned wings were now moss covered, and her pretty, flowing dust-covered dress, well she, too, would have some explaining to do.

Jack was rolling on the bank clutching his sides and trying to talk, but not managing a word. Each time he opened his mouth, he had to close it again; words simply would not form. His cheeks were flushed, his eyes filled with tears of laughter, and his sides ached.

"Boris, Jack, how could you?" Ivy screamed again as she extended her tiny arm toward Lilly, who was still sitting on top of Boris. "That was awful. We were trying to help you!" she whined, looking at the state of her dress. "Look at me. Look at us!"

Boris was trying to talk, but he was laughing too hard, and now he understood why Lilly had trouble controlling her laughter earlier. Lilly also knew how poor Boris must have felt when she was laughing at him. If she had only waited, if he had only laughed first, would that have been different? She didn't know, but she did know that it didn't feel very nice at all to have one of your closest friends laugh at you, especially when she felt so awful. To make matters worse, she looked awful, not to mention the fact that she smelt awful, too! She felt guilty for laughing at Boris in the first place and wished she hadn't been so careless with her giggles. She was a sight to look at and she stunk. Lilly wasn't quite sure what to do next.

Boris finally managed to stop laughing. He threw a slimy piece of moss playfully at Lilly, and, to his surprise, she peeled it out of her soggy hair and threw it back at him. He took a deep breath and pointed toward a boulder in front of him.

"I'll try to make my way to it and use it to ground me. Then hopefully Jack can pull me out, and together we can pull you out," he said to Lilly and Ivy. It was the only plan they had, and it was starting to get late, so it was a good plan.

Boris gingerly stood up on his feet. This time, he never raised them off the ground. Slowly he shuffled them one in front of the other toward the boulder. He went very slowly and managed to shuffle all the way to the boulder without slipping once. He leaned toward the rock and wrapped both of his arms around it. He stabilized his feet while positioning himself and called out to Jack. Jack laid flat on the bank, on his tummy, and in the slime no less, and stuck his hand out toward Boris. Ever so slowly Boris reached for Jack, and with their hands clasped tightly together, Jack pulled Boris to the bank. One final tug and Boris was face down, nose to nose with Jack in the mud. Chuckling, the little fairlings couldn't resist a quick mud fight, which lasted only until Lilly quickly reminded them of the seriousness of their situation.

"Nice one Jack," Boris said, "Now it's time to get the girls out!"

Boris held onto Jack very tightly, as Jack held onto Ivy. On the count of three, they pulled Ivy safely to the bank. Lilly was the only one left in the brook, and she was starting to shiver. Slowly she stood on her feet, the water was rushing around her, making it difficult to move. She extended her hand toward Boris, who managed to clasp it almost immediately, and after one tug Lilly was on semi-dry land. The three fairlings collapsed on top of Boris and burst out laughing. After a quick game lily pad surfing through the shallow water, it was time to get back to the patch. They were soaked, dirty, smelly, hungry and cold.

Lilly put an arm around Boris's shoulders. "You know Boris," she said, "I shouldn't have laughed at you when you fell in, that wasn't very nice and I'm sorry, I really am."

Boris blushed and tapped her little button nose. "That's okay Lilly, I'm sorry I ruined your dress – the wash monitors will be able to get that pressed properly, won't they?" he asked.

"Well of course they will," said Jack. "Have you seen the size of those heat presses they use? I keep trying to use them, but they won't let me. I asked nicely and everything. It's because of the steam, it can give a fairling a very nasty burn, or so I've been told!" He chuckled, "Although, I am just desperate to have a go!"

The four fairlings carefully made their way back to the patch, counting the fireflies as they ran through the woods. They jumped logs and darted along the curvy paths, desperately wanting to hover but knowing better than to do so on no-flight days! As they caught their breaths and their tummies rumbled, their conversation turned to supper and they discussed their favorite meals.

"I hope they have fairy dumplings today," Boris said rubbing his tummy. "I'm starving, and they always give me two helpings and extra crispy fairy rolls."

Lilly rubbed her tummy and grinned, "Stew, fairy stew. I love it, with a little fairy pudding. My favorite!"

Ivy agreed, although if she could just have her milk warmed, well that would be scrumptious. Boris's tummy suddenly grumbled so loudly that all four fairlings stopped talking and stared at it.

"Oh my," whispered Lilly, as she dug into her pocket and pulled out a very soggy lavender fairy twist. "Would you like this Boris to tide you over?" she asked. "Although I really must say, it goes against my better judgment."

"Euggghhh," said Ivy.

Jack, too, was shaking his head, and Lilly was wishing she'd thought twice about offering it, though her intentions had been good. Thankfully Boris declined. Arriving at the dorms, the four little fairlings went their separate ways; Boris and Jack to the left, Lilly and Ivy to the right. Though their clothes were still damp, their hair had dried into matted messes of tangles and moss.

"Bathing room," said Ivy, as she attempted to run her fingers through her hair with no luck at all.

Lilly nodded, "Absolutely, bathing room first!" she agreed.

The four fairlings were tired; they'd had a fabulous day.

Running through the forest, playing *hide and go seek a fairling,* lily pad racing, and even their unplanned adventure hadn't been that bad. However, it was time to bathe, eat, and sleep. Lilly was ready for all three as were her friends. Crawling into bed seemed like a treat. The dorm monitor ran through her nightly routine: roll call, bed check, tucking each little fairling in, drawing the curtains, and blowing out the candles. She took one final look around and noting that nothing was wrong or out of place, she jotted it in her log. The dorm monitor poured herself a cup of hot rose hip tea. She made sure nobody was looking, and dunked her fairy biscuits into her cup of tea. Pulling out her favorite scroll *Midnight Encounters… a Fairy Mystery,* she settled in for the evening.

2 • TRICKS IN THE CLASS-SCHROOM

The silver bell above the dorm monitor's station rang gently; it was time to start the day. Madame Louise walked between the beds and opened the curtains of every tiny window. The sunlight poured into the room. Leaning down, she whispered softly to each beautiful, sleeping little fairy.

"Good Morning precious little fairling, time to wake up," she said stroking the hair from the face of each little fairy before moving to the next bed. She leaned over and whispered into Lilly's ear, "Time to wake up, little fairling, good morning sleepy, beautiful fairy, time to wake up."

Lilly stirred, but she didn't quite wake up. She thought she heard Madame Louise's gentle voice, but she was sleeping so soundly that she was sure she was dreaming. She nestled deep under her sheets and made no attempt to get out of the bed. She was having a fabulous dream and wasn't quite ready to wake up.

Madame Louise slowly pulled back Lilly's sheets and stroked Lilly's golden curls away from her face. She stared at Lilly for a moment and smiled. Gently, she tickled her tummy, whispering as she did so.

"Lilly dear, it really is time to get up . . . you shall miss breakfast if you don't," she said with a giggle. "Breakfast, Lilly, fairy crumpets with hot butter and a lovely cup of rose hip tea. It's your favorite, Lilly," Madame Louise giggled.

Rosie, Ivy, and Pearle had gathered around the foot of Lilly's bed; they were tickling her toes and whispering her name. Lilly finally sat up and glanced at Madame Louise, who was motioning toward her. Lilly knew it was time – time for their hug. Madame Louise grabbed all four little fairies, pulled them close, and gave them a little hug to start the day. She did it every morning to each and every one. Lilly jumped out of bed and glanced at Pearle.

"May I, Pearle," she whined. "Please?"

Pearle nodded and tapped her lap. "Of course," she

giggled, "come on!"

Lilly jumped straight from the bed into little Pearle's lap. "Could you please take me to the bathing room? I have misplaced my slippers and my toes are freezing," Lilly said as she pointed to her tiny feet.

Pearle's face lit up. There was nothing she loved more than giving the girls a ride on her lap. *Pearle's Chariot,* the fairlings called it. Although Pearle used it daily, there was no slowing her down; she was incredibly fast in the chair that the elders had designed specifically for her. Often going too fast, especially around corners when playing her favorite game, make a fairling green! Spinning as fast as she could around and around on her back two wheels, trying to make the fairies sick. She could almost always make Boris sick and sometimes even Jack. Lilly, often turned grey, though not quite green, and Ivy and Rosie, well they were pros just like Pearle.

"To the bathing room," Pearle said playfully.

"To the bathing room!" All the little fairies giggled as Madame Louise looked on.

Lilly was in Pearle's lap, Ivy was running behind, and Rosie was perched on the arm of the chair. *This does not look very safe at all!* thought Madame Louise, though she never said a word. She simply listened for a moment to the beautiful sound of fairy giggles that had suddenly filled the dorm, but when Pearle's chair tipped onto one wheel, Madame Louise, could hold her tongue no longer.

"Pearle, do be careful," she said with a smile. "Slow down dear, please. I still can't believe there's so much swivel on those wheels!" She smiled as Pearle maneuvered the chair with ease, a skill she had acquired over time without complaint. Madame Louise remembered the day Monsieur Parley, with Monsieur Pierre at his side, introduced the new chariot to Pearle. She had been so pleased that her smile radiated throughout the room. *In fact,* thought Madame Louise, *I do believe it was Lilly, even then, who dove into Pearle's lap for the very first ride.* She watched as they exited the dorm and entered the bathing room, and she listened to the little fairies as they helped each other. "On the count of three; one, two, three" The group of fairlings giggled as they lifted Pearle out of her chair and placed her aside the bathing tub, and that was that. The fairlings went about their business: washing their faces, cleaning their teeth, brushing their hair, and straightening their wings. As soon as Pearle laid down her brush and straightened her wings, she was whisked up by whomever was closest and placed safely back in her chariot . . . Pearle's chariot, and the day, proceeded as normal.

The dining hall was always busy and could often be a tad loud. Announcements were made and breakfast was served. Each little fairy ate fairy crumpets and berry crepes until their tummies were full. Lavender juice and rose hip tea completed their meal. Breakfast was a very important fairling meal indeed. The rule was that a good breakfast would get their creative juices flowing and would also make them strong – at least that's what the elder Fairy who made the announcements always said.

As the fairlings left the dining hall and headed to class, the elders looked on. Each little fairy made way for Pearle's Chariot, and the hall emptied. One by one, the little fairlings went about their schedules, and the elders went about their tasks.

Lilly's first class of the morning was fairy history. She enjoyed her history class, because Monsieur Pierre, who taught both history and science, had a knack, a gift for such things. He could teach while being funny and interesting, a skill most fairlings appreciated very much. The time would fly by quickly, often too quickly. Sitting in her seat at her desk, Lilly waited patiently for her class to begin. Jack sat down in front of Lilly, and Boris sat down next to Jack. Ivy sat behind Lilly, and Pearle sat in the aisle next to Rosie. The classroom filled quite nicely, and the class would start soon.

Jack dipped his quill into his inkwell, but the well was dry. He nudged Boris and pointed with his quill to the well. "Boris, do you have your ink jar with you?" he asked "I left mine in the dorm."

Lilly was not surprised that Jack didn't have his extra supply of ink and though she didn't say it, she was almost certain that Boris didn't have his either. She waited and listened to their exchange; though she thought she probably ought not to, she did anyway.

"I do Jack, hang on a minute," Boris chuckled, and Lilly was quite surprised as Boris dug around his satchel. He raised his finger. "Hang on, it's in here, I know it's in here," he said.

Jack smiled, "Of course it is," he said, "I don't have mine, so you must have yours, right?"

Boris nodded as he continued to dig through his satchel. His hands were rummaging from left to right and now he had an odd look on his face. Lilly knew what was next. One by one Boris placed the items from inside his satchel on top of his desk: his straight edge, his scrolls, a spare quill, and a fairy roll. "Eh, that's for later," he laughed.

"A moss bomb," Jack laughed.

"That's for later too," Boris said, as he pointed to the mass of moss sitting on the desk, and then he continued to dig through his satchel, as Jack looked on.

Lilly had seen enough. She rolled her eyes and pulled out a jar of ink. She stood up, waltzed over to Jack's desk, and filled his well. She took one look at Boris's, and it was, as she had expected, near empty. She filled his too. She turned on her tiny fairy heels, waltzed back to her seat, sat down, and never said a word.

Jack and Boris took one look at their inkwells, and at Lilly, and both chuckled. Lilly was always so prepared, but they never quite seemed to be, though Boris really had been trying, or so he thought. He purposely put an extra quill in his satchel and threw in an extra scroll as well. Though one look at the scroll he placed back in his bag made him realize it wasn't the one he needed at all. *Really, really, must work on that,* he thought as Jack dipped his quill into the ink that Lilly had filled for him. Though the boys were still laughing, the rest of the mushroom had become very quiet.

Lilly was not amused. "Really Boy's," she said as she sat down, "there's nothing funny about being ill prepared for class." She rolled her eyes and folded her tiny arms, "Sssshhhh," she whispered. "Here's Monsieur Pierre."

Every little fairling in the room stood up out of their chairs and not one little voice was heard. Monsieur Pierre had appeared at the back of the room and now suddenly appeared at the front of his desk that was located in the center of the front of the room. Lowering his arms, he motioned for the little ones to sit back down in their chairs.

"Good morning young fairlings," he said softly. "I hope you all slept well, ate a wonderful meal, fed your tummies and your brains, and are ready to get started this morning."

In unison the fairlings said, "Good morning Monsieur Pierre, we slept well, we ate well and YES, we *are* ready to get started!" Everybody including Monsieur Pierre giggled; they said the same thing to each other every Monday, Wednesday, and Friday. It was then that Monsieur Pierre motioned for the young fairies to roll out their scrolls, as he wrote on the enormous board what the topic of discussion was for that morning and their assigned task for the day. The sound of the quills scraping across the paper and the taps of the quills against the inkwells were the only sounds that could be heard, until Monsieur Pierre laid down his chalk. All the little fairlings followed suit and laid their quills on their desks, sat straight up in their chairs, and got ready to pay attention. All except for Boris, who was struggling to finish writing down all of his requirements for the day. The room was quiet, except for the erratic sound of Boris's quill scraping across his scroll. He was frantically trying to write, but his quill was dry.

Impossible, thought Boris, *Lilly just filled the well up for me.* He continued to dip the quill into the inkwell – the well was dry. *It can't be,* Boris thought. *It just can't be!*

"Um, um Boris," Monsieur Pierre said, though very nicely, "are you almost done, can I continue please?"

Boris wasn't almost done, not even close, but he didn't know what to do. Without warning Monsieur Pierre appeared at Boris's side, looking down at Boris's desk and frowning.

"Can you read that Boris?" he asked, though he didn't really wait for Boris to answer him. "Why don't you slow down, take your time, and I will continue. Try to listen as best you can, um?"

Boris nodded. He took a deep breath and wiped his

brow. He wanted to continue, he wanted to write down his task, but he couldn't, he had no ink. He had no idea why he suddenly had no ink, and Monsieur Pierre was already in front of the class again, so Boris couldn't explain why he couldn't continue to write. He didn't dare.

Suddenly Boris noticed his fingers were sticky, as were his hands. Looking down he realized they were black, all black, and covered in ink. How on earth did Monsieur Pierre not notice such a thing or *maybe he had*, thought Boris. But Monsieur Pierre, once again in mid lecture, did not appear to have noticed. Boris started to panic. He couldn't write; he couldn't pay attention long enough to listen, and he couldn't leave the mushroom without drawing attention to his most dreadful situation. His cheeks became flushed as he realized his inky hands had left unsightly fingerprints all over his scroll. He looked at his desk in horror unsure of how to proceed. Wracking his brain, thinking and thinking, he wondered what had happened. There was no ink, then there was the ink that Lilly had brought him, then there was no ink again, but there was ink because it was all over him, but he didn't know how . . . and now he didn't know what to do! He had been sitting there the whole time writing, working, and doing what he was supposed to be doing and trying very hard to be a very good, studious fairling, just like Lilly, but it wasn't working and he didn't know why!

Monsieur Pierre was slightly agitated and stood once again in front of Boris. Boris's eyes were wide open, his mouth was ajar, and he had a blank expression on his face. He raised his inky hands for the professor to see. Poor Boris couldn't even talk but simply looked at his hands in disbelief and shrugged his tiny shoulders in despair. He had absolutely no idea how the inkwell had become empty and how he was wearing all of the ink that Lilly had so thoughtfully given him. He waited to see what would happen next and didn't have to wait long.

Boris held his breath, his heart pounded and his cheeks were bright red, as every fairlings' eyes were upon him. Then he heard the most unusual sound. If he was not mistaken, it was a laugh, definitely a laugh. He didn't dare turn to see where the laugh was coming from. Monsieur Pierre suddenly took two steps to the left, and stood directly in front of Jack.

Jack tried with all his might to stop laughing, but he couldn't. He was biting his tongue, sucking his cheek, and pinching his own fingers, but the laughing wouldn't stop. It was Jack who looked odd now, as his face had turned bright red from holding his breath to stop laughing.

Lilly sat with her tiny hand clasped over her mouth, as she suddenly realized what had just happened. Although she didn't know the details, she knew that Jack had something to do with Boris's predicament. *Oh Jack, I should have known,* she thought as she watched the situation unfold.

Rosie tried very hard to look over Ivy's shoulder to watch what was going on, but little Pearle, knowing full well what had happened, just like Lilly, didn't dare glance that way. She wanted to avoid eye contact at all cost with Monsieur Pierre, Boris, and Jack.

Boris, suddenly realizing what had happened stared in horror at Jack, who was wishing with all his might that he hadn't slipped so many rose hip buds into the inkwell. He had no idea so many would swell so quickly and dry up the ink. One surely must have flipped out as Boris frantically dipped his quill for ink. Boris had unknowingly put a rose hip bud underneath his fingers, causing it or maybe them to pop, spewing ink all over his hands.

"J A C K," Monsieur Pierre said, very firmly indeed. "May I have a word please with a certain mischievous little fairling, named Jack? Right now if you don't mind!"

Monsieur Pierre glanced around at the class. "We'll be right back. Revise your scrolls, please."

Jack stood up, though rather slowly, and made his way to the back of the room where Monsieur Pierre was pointing a finger, on his raised hand, toward the door. Though he didn't move very quickly, Jack was moving just the same although now he wasn't laughing at all!

Lilly's eyes met Boris's and Boris shuddered, the dust factory fresh on his mind, but this was not that bad, surely. Boris was right, after a quick scolding regarding pranks in the class-shroom, an essay due with the topic *of how to be respectful of other fairlings' property, and when it's appropriate to play jokes on his classmates,* Jack was thankful that was that. Quite relieved, Jack sat back down and glanced only briefly at Boris as he slipped the apology note onto Boris's desk that Monsieur Pierre demanded he write. Just then Boris was excused to the bathing room to wash the ink from his little plump hands and the history lesson once again got under way.

The fairlings listened intently as Monsieur Pierre discussed Sir Ian Walker IV, one of the bravest fairy settlers of the original colony. He discussed the reason Sir Ian had grown the great mushroom patch specifically where he had and why he had chosen that particular location of the forest to protect the colony. They were hidden deep in the forest beneath the foliage, close to the babbling brook, with plenty of ground to cultivate for food and without a soul knowing they were there; it was ideal. The location had grown into the magnificent colony they now enjoyed, safe and protected from the rest of the world.

Lilly listened closely as Monsieur Pierre spoke of the trials Sir Ian had endured: his limited tools, the minimal quantities of dust for tasks, and the master gnomes he used as protectors of the colony. These gnomes often helped build as well as protect the patch. Lilly was fascinated. Her eyes followed Monsieur Pierre as he talked and walked from one side of the shroom to the other, and used his hands, as he so often did, to explain the events he was discussing. She didn't want him to stop talking. She was fascinated by his words, especially the part about the mulch farm Sir Ian had developed, and was startled when the bell above the board suddenly rang. Regretfully, Lilly gathered her things.

"Well, my dears," Monsieur Pierre said, "until next time then Good day!"

"Good day," all the little fairlings said in unison as they

stood quietly behind their desks until Monsieur Pierre had left the room. Once he had, the little fairies followed suit.

"I think history must be one of my favorite classes. I think it's fascinating. Don't you?" Lilly asked Boris as she followed behind him.

Boris thought for a moment. He liked history but didn't like it as much as Lilly did. He didn't dislike it, but he didn't love it either. Now he looked puzzled. He pondered his own question as Lilly slapped him gently on the arm.

"Boris, stop it," she said with a giggle. "You don't have to love it. It wasn't really a real question I suppose." She nudged Boris gently and added, "I know full well that Flight 101 is by far your favorite lesson, and, if I'm not mistaken, Colony Exploration is Jack's favorite."

Boris laughed. Lilly was right. Jack loved to explore and one day he hoped to be a famous explorer. And Boris, well, he just wanted to fly without breaking anything like his foot or his wing or other things such as branches, mushroom tiles or anything he happened to hit while accidently flying too low or too fast or just off course. Boris wanted to hover with ease and fly with speed! Unfortunately, and much to Mademoiselle Francesca's disappointment, he just wasn't very good at it! Though he did try very hard, a point that Mademoiselle noted each time Boris took a spill. He was certain he would get the hang of it eventually; Mademoiselle had told him so!

3 • FLIGHT 101

The air was crisp but not cold. The sun was up and there wasn't a single breeze to be had, absolutely perfect flying conditions. Mademoiselle Francesca stood patiently at the front of the landing patch awaiting her young fairlings to join her. It was Pearle who arrived first *as always*, thought Mademoiselle Francesca. Mademoiselle knew Pearle couldn't wait to lift her tiny little body out of her chariot. She did it with such ease, so it was no wonder Pearle was always the first one to arrive. It was as if it were her gift to fly, thought Mademoiselle Francesca as she looked on, amused by the look on Pearle's face as she anxiously awaited the arrival of her classmates. Pearle was ahead of the class in all of her techniques, but to her credit she never showed off. She always waited until she was called upon to fly and never raised her hand to volunteer to demonstrate, but was pleased and willing when she was asked to do so. She flew so effortlessly, so gracefully, and was absolutely beautiful to watch. On that point every elder in the colony agreed.

One by one the young fairlings took their positions in the middle of the mushroom patch, known as the launching and landing site. Mademoiselle Francesca walked behind the row of little fairies, all lined up perfectly straight, waiting for their instructions. It was a well-known fact that flying was not as easy as it appeared. Most fairlings automatically assumed they had a rite of passage – perfect flight they did not. It was a skill, much like other skills, that had to be mastered, developed, and fine-tuned.

"All right then little ones are we ready? If so let's begin" Mademoiselle said as she addressed the class.

It wasn't unusual for Mademoiselle to begin Flight 101 with a few stretching exercises to limber up her class, especially after they had been sitting for so long in their class-shrooms, and stretching was always followed by a drill, a hovering drill, a very difficult task indeed.

"Two inches please little ones," Mademoiselle

instructed. "Hover only two inches off the ground – not three, not four, just two – two inches please." She observed her students and added, "As you know, two inches is far more difficult than ten to maintain in proper form, proper being the key word!"

Though two inches wasn't very high at all, it was not nearly as easy as it sounded. It required a massive amount of control, regardless of a fairling's size. It was instinctual for fairies to speed up the flapping of their tiny wings while in motion, therein lay the first problem. If their wings went too fast, their bodies automatically elevated higher, a natural reaction to increased wing speed. If their wings fluttered too slowly, their little frames lowered gently to the ground that is unless they were like Boris who always seemed to manage to plop to the ground, rather awkwardly at that.

Boris had already run into trouble, though naturally not by choice. While trying to lift his body two inches off the ground, his wing speed had increased too fast, slowing down his wings too quickly, which caused them to stop completely. Not a move Boris had contemplated when he plopped to the ground.

Fortunately, Mademoiselle Francesca was both gracious

as well as polite. She managed to look the other way and address the class as poor Boris jumped to his feet. Standing back in position, Boris tried again. Fluttering his wings at what he believed was medium speed, he took a deep breath and began to hover off the ground. Mademoiselle turned her attention directly towards Boris. Standing behind him she gently pulled his shoulders back and then stepped back to observe.

Boris flapped and fluttered his wings feeling as though he were several feet off the ground, although he knew he was only a couple of inches in the air, he struggled to stay upright. His little tummy pulled him forward, though unintentionally. His wings were tiring and fluttering too slowly and then too fast, as he attempted to support his crooked form. His cheeks were flushed, and he gasped for air. It was hard work, hovering correctly, or even trying to hover correctly, since Boris was certain he wasn't doing it properly at all.

"Boris dear," Mademoiselle Francesca whispered softly, "You are almost trying *too* hard – if there is such a thing." She stepped toward him and pulled him gently back to the ground.

"Here, try this," Mademoiselle said as she took her

hand and gently raised his chin. "Watch me dear," she whispered. "It is true that you are working very hard, but because you are trying so hard, your little body cannot relax and your wings are tiring so."

Boris thought about that for a moment. His wings were tired, and he had been trying, but if he wasn't trying, and his wings didn't flutter so fast, how would he hover? He had no idea. Boris was very confused.

Mademoiselle Francesca simply smiled at Boris as she hovered straight up into the air two inches with ease. Her wings never moved, and Boris noticed this immediately. His eyes grew huge. How had he not noticed that before? The elders did that all the time. They appeared, disappeared, hovered, flew up, down, and around. He must have just overlooked the fact that sometimes they engaged their wings and sometimes they did not!

Mademoiselle Francesca lowered herself back to the ground straightened the wrinkle that had formed in her dress with her hands, smiled at Boris and said, "Now dear, you try."

Lilly was concentrating very hard as Mademoiselle walked behind her. She took a deep breath, held her little head high, relaxed her shoulders, wiggled her toes, wiggled her fingers, closed her eyes, and started to flutter her wings. Slowly her body began to rise off the ground and she opened one eye. Lilly took a peek. She had thought that she was in the correct position, but she had to be sure. Realizing it was hard to see clearly through one eye, she opened the other and glanced toward the ground.

"Very nice dear," a familiar voice from behind her said. "Just a little more speed in those tiny wings if you please," Mademoiselle said softly, as she continued down the row of fairlings.

Slowly, Lilly increased the speed of her wings, one flutter at a time, a little faster every other flutter. As usual, Mademoiselle had been right. Lilly found herself in perfect position and she couldn't be more pleased. She was after all trying very hard and finally it had paid off, because Mademoiselle Francesca had noticed. Lilly tried not to smile too big as she maintained the position that she had been told was the correct one, but she was very pleased with herself indeed.

"That's it dear," Mademoiselle Francesca said with pride. "Pearle, you too. Your form is perfect as usual. You are clear, dear, to fly above the tall grass," she said as she continued down the row of fairies who tried to hover only two inches off the ground. Glancing again at Lilly she added, "Lilly, you may also fly the tall grass. Ivy, you may go. Rosie, please continue to hover. Boris, of course, continue to try to hover. And Jack, this is your last warning, lower, please!"

Mademoiselle watched her little flyers for a moment before she addressed the young fairlings who were still having difficulties on the flight row.

"May I have your attention please . . . Jack that means you too," she said without actually looking at him, and Boris couldn't help but wonder how on earth she did that.

"Do you all see, dears? Do you see how little Pearle glides with ease over the tops of the tall grass?" Mademoiselle said pointing to Pearle.

"Why it will not be long before she is strong enough to clear the treetops," she giggled as she turned her attention slowly toward the opposite end of the row. Very discreetly Mademoiselle wandered toward Boris and whispered in his ear as she corrected his position, "Clear them correctly I should say, um Boris?" Smiling she tapped the tip of Boris's little button nose and slowly continued to walk the row.

"Jack, Jack… JACK!" Mademoiselle Francesca said,

though by the time she had repeated his name for the third time, her voice was definitely louder. Lilly was certain of it.

Startled by the sound of Mademoiselle's voice, Jack stopped flying and hit the floor, quite hard at that. Though they wanted to giggle no one dared, remembering their *P's & Q's Manners & Rules class, via Rule Number 11, embarrassing another fairy purposely or laughing at an inappropriate time, such as at a fairy and not with a fairy, is very rude indeed.* All of the fairlings knew that polite little *fairies tried very hard never, ever to be deliberately rude!*

Mademoiselle Francesca suddenly appeared in front of Jack. A quick once over of his little frame assured her he was all right and then the scolding began.

"You were not cleared to fly, Jack. Fairies don't fly until cleared, and they're not cleared until I clear them!" Mademoiselle said firmly.

Boris tried really hard to avoid looking at Jack, but he couldn't help it. As soon as he heard Jack hit the ground and then watched him jump to his feet, he had glanced that way. A mistake, Boris was sure of it, as soon as his eyes met Jack's. Biting his cheek and looking at his feet, Boris tried not to laugh. Rule 11 of the *P's & Q's, Manners & Rules,* was on his mind. Boris turned toward Lilly for help, but she was still in flight and unable to assist. Boris was alone. Focusing on the ground, he decided not to look at Jack, again, but to count the leaves that lay at his feet instead. His eyes located a leaf. He counted it, and then located another and another, but Boris just had to do it. He had to glance one last time at Jack. He didn't want to, but he did it anyway. Boris looked up at the very same time Jack did. Jack's eyes met his and though he tried not to, he completely lost it. Boris chuckled until his chuckling turned to laughter along with Jack's.

Mademoiselle Francesca wasn't having it! By the scruffs of their necks, she pulled Boris and Jack from the flight row and set them aside. One look from her normally gentle face, that now bore a scowl, told them she was not pleased. Pointing her finger at them both, she assured them they would be grounded for the rest of the week!

Boris's heart sank, even though he knew he deserved it. Why had he looked at Jack? He was still trying not to giggle. He didn't know what was so funny . . . except it was Jack. Boris turned the other way, shaking his head, deliberately not looking at Jack and hoping against hope that he could just stop laughing.

Mademoiselle Francesca took a deep breath, hovered

six inches off the ground, spun around, and faced the rest of the class. She paused momentarily before speaking, but when she did speak each and every fairling gave her their full attention. Mademoiselle's patience was running thin, and they were well aware of it.

"May I have your attention please?" Mademoiselle Francesca asked. "I believe we all know why Boris and Jack have been grounded, so I will not waste my time or your time discussing it."

No one said a word. They just listened as she spoke.

"Now let's get back to work," she said as she walked slowly down the row of fairies. "I would like to share a little tip with the class. Some of you naturally know how to hover and fly without knowing that you know how do to it, but others are struggling, and this tip will be very helpful, indeed, so please pay attention. I will only say this once."

All eyes and ears were upon Mademoiselle, but Lilly couldn't help but wonder if she knew how to do whatever it was. She wasn't sure but wanted to know, as did the others. Pearle sat back in her chariot, Ivy held Rosie's hand, and Jack kicked dirt at Boris, though no one saw him.

Boris knew immediately he fell into the category of *needs help*, but he didn't mind. He wanted to fly so badly and he had learned that after crashing through the treetops and landing on the forest floor, that he needed quite a lot of help. He was already regretting the actions that had led to his grounding and knew he would be miserable all week, but still his ears perked up as Mademoiselle spoke to the class. Boris even managed to ignore Jack, as Jack mouthed the words "*Mademoiselle is talking to you*," and then chuckled.

Mademoiselle Francesca began to speak. "My dears," she said, "if you only knew what I know, and in time you will, your flight transition would become effortless much like little Pearle's." She smiled and glanced at Pearle and continued to speak. "If like Pearle you did not know the weight of your own body when you flew, you would levitate with ease, for the only thing on the forefront of your mind would be the task at hand." Staring at the faces of the little fairies before her, who were hanging onto each and every word that she spoke, she continued softly.

"You are making it harder than it needs to be little ones, but you know not why or how to stop, so I will try to help you. If you take a deep breath, clear your mind, forget momentarily that you have wings and that your wings are doing the work, they will just . . . do the work!"

Every one gasped! *Forget they have wings*? Was that even

possible?

"Your wings will do what they're supposed to do, they just will, so stop trying to make them!" Mademoiselle said observing the confusion upon the faces of the young fairlings before her. The class listened with awe; they were captivated. Mademoiselle Francesca always spoke with such tenderness as she taught: her instructions never failed, and her methods were incredible, at least to Lilly.

"Though you don't mean to, you flutter your wings immediately . . . stop it!" she instructed firmly.

The class was stunned and stopped fluttering their wings! How on earth could they levitate off the ground? No flutter. No wings. No flight! There had to be more, Mademoiselle was surely not through with the lesson of the day. Ivy squeezed Rosie's hand, and Rosie glanced very quickly at Lilly, but Lilly never took her eyes off of Mademoiselle Francesca as she continued to speak.

"Pearle," she said motioning with her hand toward Pearle, "does not know the weight of her little body, ever!"

All the fairies glanced toward Pearle. None of them had ever thought about that, though they supposed they knew it to be true. It had just never crossed their minds that Pearle had no idea how the weight of her body felt, especially since each of them were reminded of it every time they tried to hover.

"Because Pearle never thinks about the weight of her little, tiny, perfect body, it is never on her mind," stated Mademoiselle Francesca as she looked up and down the line as she spoke. Each and every fairy was listening very intently. She had their full attention and continued.

"Since she never thinks about it, her mind is free and clear, and it is not an issue. She simply says in her mind to hover and she does . . . perfectly, I might add," she said extending her hand toward Pearle, who was suddenly embarrassed that she felt so proud.

Mademoiselle was not quite through. "If each and every one of you clears your mind, and *STOPS THINKING OF THE TASK AT HAND, HOVERING, IT WILL COME!*"

Still having a captive audience, she concluded her lesson, "Once you have left the surface that you are standing upon, it is then that you may straighten your back, lower your shoulders, suck in your tummy, hold your head high, and gently start to flutter your wings . . . *but*, without a single thought. *Just do, don't think*. Any questions?"

There weren't any questions, the young fairlings were stunned that they had never considered flying without thinking. Smiling at the young scholars that stood before her, Mademoiselle Francesca levitated a perfect two inches off the ground.

"Until next time," she said. "We shall hover with no wings or at least shall attempt to flutter without thinking!" and then Mademoiselle Francesca simply disappeared.

The chatter started immediately, not knowing at all how they were supposed to do such a thing. Jack shoved Boris playfully, as Boris shrugged his shoulders and examined his wings. Lilly couldn't even find the words. It was Ivy that finally spoke.

"I'm starving," she said. "To the dining hall?" Everyone agreed that was a fabulous idea!

4 • THE RACE IS ON

The dining hall was a very busy place with bustling fairies everywhere. Fairies standing in queues patiently waiting to receive their food, fairies clearing off their tables when they were through, and fairies washing their hands at the basins; they were all overseen by the dining hall monitors, who were put in place to ensure all things ran smoothly and to assist if need be. Reminding the youngsters of their manners at all times, but above all, the monitors kept fairy play to a minimum. It was Lilly who noticed that Boris was not his usual self, as she watched him picking at his fairy cress sandwich and fairy crisps – very unusual for Boris. He had an odd look on his face as well, Lilly was certain of it! She finally asked him if there was something the matter; there was, he was very worried indeed. Mademoiselle's instructions had left him puzzled, but he didn't want to think about it per her instructions. He was confused at best. His friends tried desperately to cheer him up – to take his mind off of the matter that was troubling him.

"It's all right Boris," Jack chuckled. "Just try to put the whole thing out of your mind and concentrate on something else, like exploring, or hide and go find a fairy or something."

Lilly actually agreed with Jack, since there was absolutely no point in worrying about it. And besides, as Lilly pointed out, they had both been grounded for a week anyway. Worrying served no purpose at all, except to torment poor Boris's mind.

Boris thought about their advice for a moment – he liked it. He liked it a lot! Right then and there he decided he wasn't going to think about Flight Class 101. He would forget about how to use his wings or hover two or ten inches for that matter; he was putting it to bed, so to speak, at least for now.

"Ah, I'm so glad you said that Jack," Boris mumbled, finally taking a bite out of his sandwich. "I feel better already!" He smacked his lips and took another bite of his fairy cress sandwich. "Umm, this is so good," he said, "and you, too, Lilly, thank you for agreeing with Jack. I'm starving and didn't know it and that doesn't happen very often," he laughed.

Lilly gently tossed Boris her fairy biscuit, for which he was very grateful, and Jack slid his hand into his trouser pocket and pulled out a couple of sacks of fairy delights. There was a hair squashed in one, but they were still Boris's favorite.

"I thought I'd eat two of these, but I've changed my mind. Do you want them?" Jack offered, as he slid the delights toward Boris's plate. Turning to Lilly, he offered the other packet. "You may share mine Lilly, if you like," he said with the biggest grin on his face, knowing that she would say no. They didn't look very good at all and were a tad more squished than he had originally thought. "Sorry about that. I didn't know they were so bad off!" said Jack.

Lilly thanked Jack but he was right. She took one look at the smashed bag of fairy delights and passed, politely of course. They finished their meal, cleared their table, and checked the large clock that hung high above the dining hall. They still had time to play, and climbing seemed to be the game of choice. They didn't have time to play hide and go find a fairy, since Jack was too good at it, and it was quite possible they wouldn't find him in time. They had just eaten, so go leap a fairy was out of the question. They didn't have time to play in the woods and still get back in time, and there was no time to get wet, so rock climbing was perfect.

"To the large rock then," Lilly said walking toward the door, "the one on the opposite side of the brook closest to the forest edge."

Boris and Jack knew exactly which rock Lilly was referring to, perfect for rock climbing. As they left the hall, the monitor checked their hands one by one. Jack was sent back to rewash his hands, *no surprise there,* thought Lilly, though she didn't say it. Running toward the brook, they met Ivy and Rosie and invited them to join in, *the more the merrier* was always the fairy way! Rosie and Ivy were very pleased with the invitation and willingly accepted.

Lilly counted to three, the race was on. Jack was fast, but Ivy was faster much to Jack's disappointment. Though Jack tried very hard to outrun her, he just couldn't seem to pass her.

Rosie giggled as she ran. Being a terrible runner, she

passed only Boris, though Boris walked half the way and kept saying, "By choice, by choice. "

"I prefer to stroll," Boris said, "or to fly, which as you all know I'm not quite cleared to do as of yet anyway, but hopefully soon, though not soon enough for me!"

Rosie stopped and waited for him and Lilly waited for them both, while Ivy and Jack waited up ahead at the foot of the rock. Playfully they nudged each other and the challenge was on. Which little fairy would get to the top of the rock first? Ivy had won the foot race; she was determined to win the climb!

"Here are the rules," Jack said staring down Ivy. "You can't stop. You can't take your hands off the rock, EVER. No scratching your nose, moving your hair or wiping sweat off your face. If your hands leave the rock, you are eliminated. Any questions?"

He looked at each face and saw there were none. The rules were straightforward and sounded quite fair; they were all anxious to get started before they ran out of time. It was Ivy that asked the big question.

"Who's going to count us off?"

"Um," Jack said laughing, "well not *YOU*!"

"Nor *YOU*," said Ivy with a giggle of her own.

"I will," said Lilly, and everyone agreed that was a fabulous idea.

Boris took a position at the base of the rock as did Rosie, right next to Boris. Jack checked out a different portion of the rock but didn't like it, so he walked back. He ran his hand up and down the surface of his new position and decided it would work. Ivy couldn't help but smile as she watched Jack try to find the perfect spot. He was so serious. She stood next to Rosie but kept her eye on Jack. Lilly walked to the end of the row and began the countdown.

"One go a fairy, two go a fairy, three go a fairy and we're off!" she hollered as loud as she could. As soon as the last count was called, one by one Lilly, Boris, Jack, Ivy, and Rosie scrambled as fast as they could up the face of the giant rock, not once taking their hands off of the rough surface while they carefully looked for the next ridge, jagged edge, or place to set their feet.

Jack and Ivy glanced at each other every now and then with their game faces on. Boris, however, was just enjoying the fresh air and the climb itself.

Rosie also climbed casually up the rock, as did Lilly, enjoying the scenery and smiling at each other if their eyes happened to meet. Boris continued to climb, carefully placing his hands and feet. Jack was moving at an incredible rate of speed for a fairling who had just eaten lunch, but Ivy was right behind him. Playfully she teased him. "I'm right behind you," she giggled. "I'm about to pass. You'll have to give me room."

Jack couldn't stand it. He stopped for a moment, checking behind him; Ivy had tricked him. She wasn't on his heels, for which he was incredibly grateful. Winking at Ivy, he started his climb up the rock once again as fast as his legs would carry him. His eyes scanned for his next move, as his hands reached for nooks and crannies and his feet worked the slab – losing was not an option.

As Boris moved slowly up the rock, his little nose started to itch right on the tip. He wiggled it as best he could, but it didn't help. He pressed his face against the cold slab; it felt good, as he scratched his face up and down on the rock, until a tiny sliver of slate stuck him in the nose.

"Ouch," cried Boris, "that hurt!" Instinctively his hand left the rock and grabbed his nose. He was out of the race though he didn't seem to mind, because a break was just what he needed. Once assured that Boris was all right, everyone continued up the slab of rock, though Boris had noticed his little nose had started to throb.

Lilly continued to move up the wall slowly, but still upward. Ivy and Jack were neck and neck, racing every inch of the way. Rosie hummed as she climbed without a care in the world, like Boris and Lilly, the climb was more important than the race.

"Boris," Lilly called from above, "Look how high I am. I don't think I've managed to climb so high before. This is really high for me!" Lilly felt very proud of herself; she typically didn't climb so high, quite an accomplishment. She stopped momentarily for a break, the air had chilled, and she noticed clouds were rolling in from the west.

"Boris is it supposed to rain today?" she asked.

Boris looked toward the west. It was definitely darker that way. He had not read the weatherboard before they had left the patch, there didn't seem to be a need, since the weather had been perfect when they left. He shrugged his shoulders; he didn't know, but it certainly looked as if it might rain. He pointed to the west and then pointed toward Jack, Ivy, and Rosie, "I think as soon as they reach the top, we should play it safe and go back to the patch," he said, "If a storm is brewing, we don't need to be out here!"

Lilly and Rosie agreed. As soon as the race was over, they would head back. Lilly looked up the rock, but Jack was nowhere in sight. She stuck out her hand and caught tiny grains of dust that fell from the garments of Jack and Ivy. They sparkled and danced in the palm of her hand, and she was reminded of the factory, Liam, and the foreman. Carefully, she placed as much of the dust as she could catch in her pouch – never waste the dust she told herself, never! A lesson learned and never taken for granted, she was quite pleased she had just saved the dust from waste. After all, the colony worked very hard to produce the precious fairy dust she had just saved. *Time well spent,* thought Lilly as her mind drifted to the factory. *Time well spent,* she thought, *Time Well Spent!*

Boris placed his little hand over his eyes as he watched Lilly catching the dust as Rosie continued climbing the rock. Though he didn't say it, he was getting a little nervous as the clouds rolled in. Jack was too high to see, as was Ivy now. Lilly was tired and realized for the first time, since she had been saving the dust, that she was out of the race anyway. Rosie had finally had enough. She raised a hand as she sat down on a ledge.

"I'm done," she said. "I'm tired." And with that she

made her way back toward Boris, who had found a lovely ledge of his own to sit on while he waited for the others.

Though Lilly had already lost her position in the race, she proceeded to put one hand in front of the other, one at a time. Moving her feet one at a time slowly up the wall, she realized she was feeling tired. Looking down at Boris and Rosie, she wondered if she were ready to quit climbing. But wasn't she going to try to get to the top? She decided no, she was definitely too tired; time to head back down, and that's exactly what she did.

"I'm done as well," she giggled. "Boris, Rosie, make room for me. Fairy coming down!"

Sitting on the ledge, the three little fairies waited patiently for Jack and Ivy to join them. They couldn't see who had reached the top first, they wondered if it would be Jack or would it be Ivy? Boris was certain Jack would make it to the top first, and Lilly and Rosie had to agree with him. Jack was an incredible climber. After several minutes, Ivy finally started back toward the ledge. Jack had won, but it had been a fantastic race. Flopping down next to Lilly, Ivy gasped for air.

"I almost had him," Ivy said in between breaths. "I really did. For just a second I thought I was going to win, but you know Jack," she smiled as she looked up toward Jack, making his way down the rock toward them. "Nice one Jack, you deserved that one . . . but maybe, just maybe I'll catch you next time!"

Though he wasn't supposed to, Jack hovered the rest of the way down. "I thought she had it, I really did," he said as he perched on the ledge with the others. "Ivy, I'm certain you will catch me next time!" he said, and really meant it.

The four little fairies took a quick break together on the ledge to admire the spectacular view, high above the tall grass that overlooked the babbling brook. Soon it would be time to get back to the patch; afternoon classes were about to begin. One by one they carefully made their way off the ledge and down the rock, but going down they did not dare race. Each little fairling looked out for the other, asking every now and then if the other was doing all right as they slowly moved downward. The rock was rough and uneven and had been much easier to navigate going upward than downward. It was Boris who jumped off the rock first, extending his hand to help Lilly, as her beautiful pink dress suddenly caught on a piece of jagged rock. Gently he lifted the hem of her skirt and released it, without a tear at that!

They ran all the way back to the patch, while jumping the dandy-lions as they came upon them. Parting at the fork leading into the center of the colony, they said their goodbyes and went their separate ways.

Lilly, Ivy, and Rosie went to fairy culinary class. Boris and Jack went to colony shop, combined with colony architectonics, a very important class indeed. Architectonics taught the youngsters the importance of structural design, order, and balance while constructing and working with delicate materials such as mushrooms. Opening the door to the shop, Jack suddenly realized he had forgotten his shop apron, a necessary requirement for the class, and he had no intentions of being caught without it. Monsieur Nigel had a very short fuse when it came to not being prepared for class. Running back to the dorm, Jack realized how tired his little legs were; all the climbing and running earlier had taken their toll. For a brief moment, he contemplated hovering but thought better of it, especially since he had already been grounded for an entire week. Jack opened the shroom door to the shop and as he feared, the class was underway.

"Nice of you to join us, Jack," boomed Monsieur Nigel. "Please come on in, and take your seat, as you can see we have started without you."

Jack was more than happy to take his seat, since all eyes were upon him, and he was feeling quite uncomfortable. He didn't dare look at Boris, who was trying to be supportive as he gave him a fairies thumb up, though Jack had not seen it. To Jack's surprise, the notes jotted on the board indicated he had been gone longer than he thought. He pulled out his scroll and quill and scrambled to catch up as best he could.

Monsieur Nigel, much to Jack's relief, recapped his opening statement. Jack was struggling; he was trying to listen and trying to write. He had heard the words structural damage, mushroom rot, and mold for sure, and he was certain he had heard reinforcement, solid beams, extra adhesive, and pins, but the more Monsieur Nigel spoke, the heavier his eyelids got.

Boris noticed immediately that Jack was drifting; the race earlier had been too much. Between his meal, the race, and the fresh air, Jack couldn't keep his eyes open. Boris desperately wanted to intervene, to help Jack, so his eyes scanned the room. Jack was to the left of him and one seat in front, and his head was bobbing back and forth. Boris gently kicked the seat in front of him, but Darwin turned around. Boris's eyes grew huge, as he shook his head left to right in the hopes Darwin would turn back around. Fortunately he did, and Monsieur had not seen him. Boris mopped his brow relieved. He had not been caught, but poor Jack was still in dire need of being awakened immediately. Tap, tap, scratch, and tap went Monsieur's chalk across the board, as he wrote down the class notes, and the fairlings jotted them down on the scrolls with their quills as fast as they could, stopping only to dip quills in inkwells in front of them.

Boris had an idea that wasn't a very good one, but it was the only one he had. If he got caught, well, he could get in big trouble. Thoughts of consequences raced through his mind, like detention and grounding from flight, 1000 Lines writing assignment, and he panicked. *Calm down, Boris,* he told himself, *Jack needs you.* Though he wished he didn't, Boris knew that Jack did. To say Jack had faded was an understatement. He was starting to make noises, gurgling noises, Boris was sure of it. The giggles that had started, assured him he was right. He had to act, and act quickly. Taking his prize teeny berry out of his pocket, Boris flung it into the air toward Jack. His accuracy did not fail him; unfortunately, he was hoping the teeny berry would land on the back of Jack's neck or his arm or even on his seat or desk or anywhere other than the place it landed. It landed smack in the middle of the back of Jack's head. Jack was awake, wide-awake.

"Ahhhhh," he cried, "What was that?" he yelled at the top of his voice. "Somebody hit me in the head and it hurt!"

All eyes turned to Boris, who had slunk down in his chair, trying with all his might to suck in his little tummy so he could sink down even lower into it. But unfortunately his little tummy hit the top of his desk and try as he may he just couldn't get low enough! It was too late. Out of nowhere appeared Monsieur Nigel standing right in front of him. He took one look at Boris and pointed to the door.

"Out, out now," Monsieur Nigel said, though to his credit rather softly Boris thought. "I shall deal with you after lessons," he added reappearing at the front of the class and continuing to write on the chalkboard, as though nothing had happened.

Boris gathered his things and slowly left the room. He tried to get Jack's attention but couldn't, because Jack was jotting down his notes; he was wide awake after all, though still rubbing the back of his head!

Standing outside the door, awaiting his fate, Boris's knees trembled. He was more than ready to be done with this day. With the exception of the rock climb, it had not gone well at all. What would his punishment be, and he was certain there would be one. He couldn't think of a single reason why throwing a teeny berry at Jack's head would have seemed like a good idea to anyone but him, and it didn't seem like a very good idea at all now! Boris suddenly felt quite ill, his stomach not well at all. Palms sweating, he loosened his collar; he couldn't breathe. He was starting to panic, he was sure of it. Leaning against the wall, he slowly counted to ten, and with each count he inhaled and then exhaled. Concentrating on his breathing, he wasn't quite prepared when Monsieur Nigel appeared before him. Boris froze, not daring to even breathe at all.

"Oh for goodness sake, relax Boris," Monsieur Nigel instructed quite firmly at that. "You must breathe Boris, it's a necessity, breathe!"

Boris suddenly gasped for air, not realizing he had held his breath for so long or that his hands and brow were perspiring. Monsieur Nigel pointed to Boris's pocket. Boris glanced down, noticed his handkerchief sticking out of his britches, pulled it out, and mopped off his brow.

"Boris," Monsieur Nigel said, "At what point would you think pegging a teeny berry at Jack's head was a good idea?" He didn't wait for Boris to answer. "Was it the moment you pulled it out of your pocket or when you actually rolled it between your fingers, prior to throwing it at Jack's scalp?"

Boris was stunned; he really hadn't given it that much thought. Jack was falling asleep and needed to be awakened. He was simply trying to help, but he hadn't. Instead, he was outside the door waiting to be dealt with! Boris was actually grateful when, once again, Monsieur Nigel spoke.

"What you did with the berry, Boris, well, wasn't very wise. You could have seriously hurt Jack or someone else for that matter, but that said, I do believe I know why you did it in the first place." Monsieur Nigel straightened Boris's collar. "Now I think we've established that you shouldn't have used the teeny berry as a means to wake Jack up, very dangerous indeed," Monsieur said. "And you did disrupt lessons, so there are consequences, Boris, you understand?" he asked.

Boris's eyes were huge; he did understand, but he had no idea that Monsieur knew his motives were of good intent. "You do sir?" he asked sincerely. "You know I was only trying to help Jack, and I wasn't trying to torment or hurt him at all?"

Monsieur Nigel pulled the prize teeny berry out of his pocket. "This one's a beauty," he said with a smile, "but let's put it on a string shall we?" He paused and added, "And you shall make up your work and clean my board for a week!" Monsieur started to walk away but stopped, turned around and said, "Oh and Boris, I think Jack owes you one, don't you?" And then Monsieur Nigel simply disappeared.

5 • ROLLED FERN SEED

Lilly loved culinary class; though it was no secret that Ivy would rather attend fairy architectonics and shop, with Jack and Boris. Lilly couldn't wait to see what dish they'd be preparing, as she opened the recipe scroll and pointed excitedly to the recipe and the task at hand.

"I've been waiting for this one," she giggled. "Rolled Fern Seed . . . in the Hole Ivy, in the Hole!"

Ivy looked at Lilly as if she'd lost her mind, but, being polite, didn't say a word, although she was certain the raised eyebrows and rolled eyes gave her true thoughts away. Immediately she apologized for not sharing the same enthusiasm and promised to try to get excited about the Rolled Fern Seed in the Hole, though she honestly didn't know how!

Lilly assured Ivy she didn't have to be as excited as she was, but if she listened very closely to Madame Charlotte, she was sure they could both learn something and that was half the fun, learning something new!

Ivy was not convinced, but promised Lilly that she would listen and learn.

"I do hope I roll the pastry right," Lilly said softly as she studied the scroll. "It's very difficult to roll and set the pastry, without tearing it I mean, Ivy."

Ivy was certain Lilly would perform the task correctly, she always did, and she didn't understand the level of difficulty at all. Prepare the pastry; roll it, and stuff it . . . done! The sketch that Lilly was studying so closely simply looked like Fern Seed in the Hole, and not a very welcoming looking dish to Ivy at that, but she knew that to Lilly it was a masterpiece that she hoped to recreate.

As Madame Charlotte entered the culinary shroom, the entire class stopped talking, stood up, and waited politely to be seated again. Once Madame greeted them, she instructed them to sit down. A quick head count assured her everyone was there and she began the lesson. Madame Charlotte was the neatest elder, though not Lilly's favorite teacher, but one she certainly respected. She spoke louder than Mademoiselle Francesca but softer than Monsieur Claude. She had long, dark brown hair pulled neatly behind her. Her gown did not glisten as much as the other elders; this would indicate she spent much more time in the class-shroom, the cooking-shroom and the baking-shroom rather than actually completing other tasks. Her tasks required little dust but more physical fairy labor or directives of. Each and every elder had a specific role. Madame Charlotte's primary role was truly one of instructing and actual baking, as well as overseeing the massive colony-baking house, which required a lot of time.

"I am very pleased to announce that today we shall be preparing and of course cooking Rolled Fern Seed in the Hole, one of my favorites I might add!" Madame Charlotte said pointing to her workbench and the utensils placed neatly upon it.

Lilly nudged Ivy and grinned knowing the class was about to get underway, Ivy couldn't help but giggle herself as an overzealous Lilly pulled out a large wooden stirrer – a very large wooden stirrer!

Ivy immediately wondered how on earth Lilly always managed to find and pull out the largest wooden stirrer possible from the drawer, but didn't say a word.

Lilly's eyes were huge as she listened very intently for Madame Charlotte to instruct the class. She was ready and though Ivy wanted to giggle she didn't dare hurt Lilly's feelings.

"Now," said Madame, "we shall fold the ingredients together, fold not stir. There is a difference, who can tell me the difference?" she asked, though she never looked up from her own preparations.

Hands shot up all about the room. Madame called upon Dahlia to answer the question, which she did, and correctly at that. Ivy was looking about the shroom watching the other fairlings. There was only one other little fairy that seemed as anxious to fold not stir, as Lilly, and that was Isabella. Isabella loved to cook as well, and often she was the only fairy in the patch whose cooking skills competed with Lilly's. Ivy scanned the scroll and waited for Lilly to tell her what to do. She had found, over time, that this worked very well, and besides, that's exactly how Lilly liked it. They had an unspoken system, and they both knew it was in place but never actually discussed it; it worked well and they were both happy with it.

"Could you please pass the measuring leaf?" Lilly asked

as she pointed to the neatly stacked leaves. "The midsized one, if you don't mind Ivy?"

Ivy didn't mind at all, trying very hard to be as serious as Lilly. Her eyes scanned the measuring leaves, and if it was up to her, she would simply grab any measuring leaf, but Lilly had specifically requested the midsized one. Ivy handed Lilly the correct leaf, and Lilly thanked her for her help, as Ivy waited patiently for the next instruction, though she did look about the room a time or two.

The sky outside was very grey and it certainly appeared as if rain might be on the way. Try as she may to concentrate on the task at hand, Ivy found she couldn't keep her mind from wandering. *If it rained, what would they do at playtime?* And then her mind jumped again; she did so love the smell of rain and when the raindrops hit the ground, they did sound so lovely. It was safe to say, Ivy could not focus at all!

"Ivy, Ivy what is wrong with you?" Lilly asked sternly. "Please pay attention. You will surely not know how to roll a fern seed!"

Ivy apologized, shook her head, and while handing Lilly a pinch of grated mineral salt said, "This is next, I think."

Lilly tossed her golden curls over her shoulder in

disgust and pointed to another smaller stirrer. "Not quite yet, Ivy, but almost . . . may I have the small stirrer please?"

Ivy actually blushed; promising Lilly she would try harder to listen to Madame Charlotte, and not the wind that had picked up outside or the raindrops she could have sworn she heard dropping softly on the roof.

As the class followed along, including Ivy, dark clouds continued to roll toward the mushroom patch. Rumblings in the distance could be heard very clearly; a storm was definitely on the way. Pearle glanced at Lilly and shuddered – to this day little Pearle hated thunderstorms. It led back to the time her chariot got stuck in the mud. She had been wet and cold before the elders realized she was not safely in the dining hall with the others. Once the elders had found her and put her in a lovely hot bath, filled her tummy with hot fairy broth, and tucked her safely into bed, it was too late. Pearle had caught the most horrible cold, complete with a temperature. It had taken weeks for her to recover. Not to mention the fact it had taken days to get her chariot out of the mud and even longer to clean the mud off. It was safe to say, Pearle did not like the rain!

Rosie, Pearle's cooking partner, put her arm around her and squeezed her gently. Pearle felt better, knowing her friends were there and understood how fearful of storms she was, and didn't judge or make fun of her. This was very comforting to Pearle, and she was truly grateful for their understanding in regards to this matter.

"No worries little ones," Madame Charlotte said as she rolled out the pastry for her fern seed dish. "It will pass shortly, I'm sure." She glanced at her students and winked at little Pearle, "You'll see dear, you'll see."

Lilly had hardly noticed the storm that was brewing outside. She was too excited about rolling the pastry for the fern seed, the most difficult part of the task. To roll the pastry without tearing it, in preparation for stuffing it with the fern seed, was not easy at all. If one were to rough the pastry would tear, but if the touch of the rolling pin were too gentle, the pastry would not spread. Once the proper shape had been acquired, laying out the fern seed came next. Wrapping the seed into the pastry, creating a beautiful little pastry package was the last step prior to sliding it into the fire pit. Lilly could hardly stand the anticipation of rolling out the pastry!

Ivy was doing her best to act excited. She was smiling and helping, helping and smiling, but her heart was not in it. Once again, her mind wandered to fairy architectonics and what Boris and Jack might be building, but she caught herself and immediately stopped, scolding herself while she was at it!

"Yeahhh," she said, "roll the fern seed Lilly, you do it… I'll hand you the rolling pin," Ivy said with as much enthusiasm as she could possibly muster.

"Do I detect a hint of sarcasm, Ivy?" Lilly giggled but felt awful for asking such a ridiculous question. It was after all Rolled Fern Seed in the Hole, and though she knew culinary lessons weren't Ivy's favorite, seriously, who could resist Rolled Fern Seed . . . in the Hole! The fern seed had been rolled, stuffed, and put back together; everything went well. Once the dish was prepared, onto the slate it went. The assistants opened the massive stoves and slid the dishes into the fire pit. Each pair turned over their timers and waited. Lilly loved this part, too!

The time had come to clean up their workbenches, and Ivy didn't mind tidying up the workbench. It helped the time go by faster. Waiting for the tiny grains to run through the timer, felt, at times, like waiting for snow to fall in summer . . . one would wait forever!

"Wash or dry?" Lilly asked Ivy filling the washbasin with soapy water as she tidied the workbench.

Well that was easy; give Lilly one more second and she would tell Ivy what she should do. Ivy counted it down in her head, *three, and two, and here she goes!*

"I really don't mind washing up if you don't mind drying," Lilly said with a smile, "but it's up to you, whatever you would like to do?"

Ivy didn't mind at all; she would do whatever task Lilly requested of her. After all, Lilly had practically completed the entire cooking task by herself and clean up, well that was the least that she could do. She was grateful that Lilly loved to cook, and specifically took the time to thank Lilly for working so hard on their task. She even commented on how marvelous she thought Lilly's Rolled Fern Seed in the Hole had actually turned out.

The fern roll came out of the fire pit. For the most part, all of the dishes cooked that day looked lovely. The shroom was filled with the most delightful smell, and even Ivy thought she might like to taste the roll. It would be hard for Madame Charlotte to pick the best one; there were many choices that appeared delightful. She admired all of them and was very kind with her comments.

"Why that looks lovely," Madame Charlotte said to Rosie. "A suggestion dear for next time, if you use a little more fairy grease, you should be able to obtain a little more rise in your dough . . . um."

Rosie nodded and then asked Pearle, "Dear Pearle, what on earth is fairy grease?" After all, she hadn't seen it listed in the ingredients. Pearle did not laugh, but gently explained that Madame wanted her to fold a tad longer or harder, something like that . . . there was no fairy grease to speak of but simply meant using a little more physical effort.

Madame Charlotte picked up a fork and placed a tiny bite into her mouth. Smiling, she graciously said, "Yes, dear. Let's work on that, shall we? Then we'll talk about the mineral rock you used, or how much you didn't use I should say, as it would seem, um?"

Madame Charlotte continued to make the rounds and finally stood in front of Lilly and Ivy. Lilly was anxious, she desperately wanted to please the pallet of Madame Charlotte. She thought her Rolled Fern looked very nice, but the proof was in the pudding . . . how would it taste?

"Lovely presentation, as usual, Lilly," Madame said softly. "Could you please hand me a fork dear?"

Lilly waited nervously for her critique. Ivy reached over and grasped Lilly's tiny hand, for which Lilly was very pleased.

"Superb, Lilly, and Ivy, of course!" And that was that, but it was all Lilly needed. Madame disappeared and reappeared on the other side of the room.

The day had gone well and all of the little fairlings were worn out. Chatter in the dining hall was surprisingly minimal, possibly due to the approaching storm, thought Monsieur Pierre. He walked between the rows checking hands as the fairlings stood up to leave. It was Boris that was sent back to the washbasin twice before being allowed to leave the hall. This surprised even Boris; usually Jack was the only fairy ever sent back twice in one sitting. Boris stared at his hands, he was convinced they were stained from shop earlier and not really dirty at all, but back to the washbasin he went. Since everyone was tired, the thought of a hot bath and a cozy bed was a welcoming one. They parted in front of the study hall: Lilly, Ivy, and Rosie to the left, and Boris and Jack to the right.

Jack jumped onto Boris as they walked down the path to the dorm. "Leap a fairy, your turn," he laughed, knowing Boris couldn't resist one last game before bed. They played leap a fairy all the way to the dormitory until Boris suddenly felt ill; no doubt due to playing leap a fairy on a full tummy,

Jack thought.

Another day in the mushroom patch, though you would never know it. No one would! Hidden from the rest of the world, deep in the forest, time in the patch often seemed to stand still. There would be enough time for the fairlings to consider time, but not now . . . not inside the patch. Maybe out in the world if they were assigned outside duties, but in the mushroom patch time seems to stand still, and that's just how the elders like it.

6 • NONSTOP RAIN

The rain finally started, the thunder rolled above the patch. Lilly soaked in her bathing tub and listened as the rain hit the roof of the bathing shroom. The sound was making Lilly very sleepy; there was something quite comforting about the drip, drop, drip, drop of rain hitting the roof. She started to doze off, and was quite startled when Madame Louise gently shook her shoulders.

"Lilly, NO dear, time to get out of the bather, you're falling asleep." She smiled as she handed Lilly a lovely warm towel. "Now dear."

Lilly did as she was told, and it occurred to her that was the very reason the elders monitored the bathing room. Falling asleep while bathing could be very dangerous, indeed, she shuddered at the thought!

The usual bedtime chatter from outside the dorm could be heard, fairies giggling as they jumped into their beds. Madame Louise drew the curtains and blew out the candles. Lilly's sheets were drawn, and sleepily she slid between them. They were cool and soft, and she was certain she couldn't possibly stay awake as Madame Louise read a chapter of *Where Did Dante, the Naughty Fairy Go?* Although Lilly couldn't wait to find out where Dante had gone, no sooner had Madame Louise opened the scroll to read, and Lilly fell fast asleep.

She awoke the next morning to the sound of Pearle rattling in between the beds, her chariot clanging on the shroom floorboards. Pearle always woke up in a fabulous mood, a trait admired by everyone.

"Come on sleepy head time to get up," Pearle giggled tugging on Lilly's sheets. "I'll take you to the bathing room if you like . . . would you like a ride that is?"

Lilly had not gotten that far. Her bed was warm, and she was still sleepy. She lay there for a moment, and Pearle was already on her way. It was still raining. Had it rained all night? It was Mademoiselle Francesca that suddenly made the announcement that took everyone by surprise.

"May I have your attention please, over here, for just a moment please," she said as she waited patiently for everyone to gather around her. She smiled at each and every one of them, while gently touching the tops of their little heads before speaking again.

"It appears we have a little problem," she said.

The ears of the little fairies perked up, as they listened to what Mademoiselle had to say.

"As you can see, it's still raining and has rained all evening, at times quite heavily." She paused and looked at the faces of the little ones; they weren't quite sure what to think yet. It had rained many times before and would likely rain more, since the rainy season was just about upon them. So what could the problem possibly be?

"First and foremost, Flight 101 has been cancelled. The landing patch is flooded and since the brook is rising faster than we had expected, due to erosion, the master elders have asked that we issue a free day." The fairies looked puzzled, at best, and Mademoiselle continued. "They're issuing the free day in order to assess the current situation, any questions?"

Needless to say, there were many questions, especially via Lilly. Had there always been a problem, she asked, that they weren't aware of until now? Mademoiselle assured the fairlings that the master elders and the engineers were well aware of the erosion situation, and that it wasn't new to them. They were cancelling the lessons merely because at this time the elders were needed for other things.

Mademoiselle Francesca continued, "Now, this would be a fabulous opportunity to leaf raft or stream race, on the paths of course. Stay away from the brook, which is not a safe place to be right now!" She raised her hand to her mouth and shushed the excited little fairies. "Listen please; this is very, very important. There will be dire consequences for any fairy that does not listen . . . have fun, stay safe, and stay together in groups," she glanced at Lilly and winked. "Stay away from the brook, it is not safe, and we are assessing the situation." She turned to Madame Louise, who stood at her side, whispered in her ear, and simply disappeared.

Lilly wondered if anyone else had noticed how Mademoiselle Francesca's tunic had glistened so – all covered in dust, fairy dust. It was a sure sign of how busy Mademoiselle had already been. Lilly's feet had barely touched the ground that morning, and yet the way Mademoiselle's tunic had glistened indicated that she must have completed a handful of tasks and deeds before dawn! Lilly knew that when Mademoiselle went back to the dusting parlor, she would stand under the dust blower and all of the remaining dust on her tunic would be blown off, swept up, and reused. She only hoped she could work as hard someday!

The fairies were very excited as they ran about the dorm trying to find matching Wellington boots and raincoats. It wasn't easy with so many tiny feet to accommodate. Madame Louise couldn't help but smile as she watched them bustle about wishing she, too, could leaf raft. *So much fun*, she thought as she helped Rosie pull up her boots.

"One last thing," Madame Louise said as she stood in front of the door. "If you hear the clapping of the clouds then the flashing in the sky is sure to follow, so you must, must come in . . . do you understand?" she asked adding, "Safety, safety, safety, safety first always, or the director will cite me for sure!" She giggled, stepping out of the way; arm extended toward the door, and dismissed them to play!

It was Monsieur Pierre that had the very same conversation with Boris, Jack, and the others in the dormitory. The only difference was that he specifically told his group to play gently and nicely with the others, stressing gently.

"Jack, Boris that means you," he had said quite firmly.

Boris wasn't quite sure how to take that, was it because he was so strong? Maybe? He decided that must be it, after all, he was growing so fast.

"Let's be sure to challenge Lilly, Ivy, and Rosie to a leaf rafting race." Jack said as his eyes gleamed. "With your, shall we say, girth and strength, Boris, we're sure to win!"

Boris wasn't quite sure what Jack meant by that statement either, but he knew that Jack meant well, and he himself had not once been accused of saying things correctly. Jack ran toward the wardrobe to find the Wellingtons. Pulling out Wellington after Wellington, he finally found a matching pair, and being the very nice fairy that Boris knew that he was had found a pair for Boris first.

"Thanks mate," Boris said pulling on the Wellingtons that were just a tad too tight, but he didn't say anything since Jack had so kindly found them in the first place.

Jack finally found a pair for himself. The two of them threw on their raincoats and raced out the door with the others. Zeraz accidently stumbled and slid smack into Boris, who found himself squished between Zeraz, a wall, and what seemed like an out of control mob of fairies racing toward the door.

"Oh Boris, I'm so sorry," Zeraz said. "Here, let me help you," he offered helping Boris to his feet.

Boris decided it would be best if everyone else went first… there were plenty of leaves, no need to get hurt or cited by a safety director for unsafe play before he had even had a chance to play leaf raft.

Jack was nowhere in sight, but Boris had a feeling Jack would have picked out two leaves, and he was right. By the time Boris had made his way down the flooded path, Jack had picked out two prize leaves and twigs for oars to boot! Boris's eyes lit up, Jack had picked a couple of beauties!

"Hurry Boris, I can't wait to give them a go," yelled Jack as Boris ran toward him.

They took the leaves and waited for a spot in the newly formed stream as the other fairies including Lilly, Ivy, and Rosie floated by them. Once the coast was clear, Jack stepped onto his leaf and off he went! Carefully he used his twig to guide him in and out of the other rafters as Monsieur Nigel, and Monsieur Pierre looked on; all appeared well.

"Come on Boris, jump on," hollered Jack, now notably

way down stream!

Boris wasn't sure, but it seemed as if the flow of the water was faster than before. He waited, took his time, let the others go by, and then very carefully stepped onto his leaf. His leaf sunk a tad more than Jack's in the middle, but Boris was certain that was because he had just had a growth spurt! He was quite surprised that he actually managed to pass Lilly, who really didn't appear to mind that she was moving rather slowly as compared to everyone else. Lilly so enjoyed flowing down the stream on the leaf that it hadn't actually occurred to her to race. Ivy on the other hand was on a mission, trying very hard to track down Jack. It wasn't working. Jack had already run out of stream and was dragging his leaf and twig back up to the top of the path. Ivy had her work cut out for her; Jack wasn't about to let her win anything, including a leaf-rafting race.

"Boris, hurry up," Jack cried as Boris passed by, "Ivy's coming. We'll wait for Lilly and race!"

Boris was definitely in, though he hardly expected to win. Ivy was fast and Jack was faster, but he might be able to beat or, at the very least, tie Lilly. He was hopeful, though he didn't mention that to Lilly.

Lilly jumped off of her leaf and held out her hand,

grabbing Boris's arm so he could slow down. Boris suddenly felt quite ashamed that he was on a mission to beat Lilly in the upcoming race; he felt the urge to say something.

"Lilly," he said, "you don't mind do you when I try really hard to win the races that we're in together?"

Lilly pulled Boris safely to the path and looked at him rather oddly. "Mind," she said, "well of course not Boris, it's a race . . . though I may not win; I shall try too!" She giggled, "But it's all in fun . . . unless you're Jack or Ivy!"

Boris laughed; that was funny, true, but funny! He thanked Lilly for her hand and together they walked up the hill. They were startled by the voice that said, "Hello little ones may I have a go?"

It was Liam, the foreman's right hand helper from the dust factory. Boris suddenly became very nervous, but he didn't know why.

"I won't break it Boris, just a quick go," Liam chuckled as he reached for the leaf.

Boris suddenly panicked, did Liam read his mind . . . he was just thinking that! Liam assured him that he wasn't reading his mind, but that when he was a young fairling and the elders wanted his leaf, he surely worried they might break or ruin it! Boris was relieved, after all the explanation had made perfect sense. Proudly he handed Liam his leaf.

Liam picked out his spot on the stream. He charged the leaf in a manner the young fairlings had never seen before. To their amazement, he skimmed the surface of the stream with ease and maneuvered in and out of the fairies on the water as if they weren't even there! He wore a smile that they had not seen before either; he looked very happy, which made them happy! Out of nowhere the foreman appeared. All the fairies jumped, startled, since their eyes had been on Liam.

Lilly blushed, "Oh I'm so sorry, you startled me," she said.

The foreman smiled and gently tickled her. "No worries," he said. "I forget sometimes that you little ones are still learning." He chuckled as he watched Liam fly across the water on Boris's leaf!

"Would you look at Liam?" he asked. "What a show off, watch this," he said turning to Lilly. "May I borrow your leaf?"

Ivy was speechless; it was rare to see the foreman at all, let alone skirting across the water on a leaf. Liam spotted the foreman and the race was on! Jack giggled and pointed as the foreman began to catch up, but it was no use, for Liam had too much of a head start. He won with ease, and stepped off the leaf with the tiniest grin on his face.

"Next time, foreman," he whispered, as he patted the foreman on his back. "I'm certain of it!"

The foreman chuckled, "Liam, even if there is a next time, you will still win, I'm certain of it," he said turning to the young fairies watching in awe. "Did you see how Liam maneuvered that leaf, impressive was it not?"

Everyone agreed that it was impressive to say the least. The foreman and Liam thanked Lilly and Boris for allowing them to take a turn, and then they simply disappeared.

"You know, they're very busy the foreman and Liam," Lilly said softly, "but did you see how much fun they had?"

Boris picked up his leaf and ran back toward the newly formed stream. The path was no longer in view. Very carefully he found the perfect spot to place his leaf, in between the fairies and large splashes. A gust of wind indicated that the storm was getting closer, and soon the elders would instruct playtime to be over. Boris lunged for the leaf; he made it, though shakily at best. Lilly, Ivy, and Rosie ran to the edge of the water, racing with Boris, as he skimmed over the water dodging in and out of other rafters.

"Move over Boris," Jack yelled, "I'm coming with you!"

Boris carefully moved to the middle of the leaf, and once Jack was in position he would then move to the front of the leaf. Boris steered the leaf to the edge as best he could. The wind had definitely picked up, and Boris appeared to be having difficulties with his navigational skills.

"A little closer, Boris," Jack hollered, "just a little closer."

Boris maneuvered the leaf over the tiny-formed waves; slowly but surely he found himself in the most perfect position for Jack to join him. Jack ran as fast as he could, and with a great big lunge he leapt toward the leaf. Just as Jack leapt into the air, Boris repositioned himself, moving to the front of the leaf. It was unusually perfect timing for Boris, and Lilly was certain that even Boris was surprised. Down the stream the two went with Lilly, Rosie, and Ivy no longer able to keep up. Out of breath, they watched Boris and Jack ride the leaf down the stream all the way to the bottom of where the path was supposed to be. Just as they stepped off their leaf, the bell rang, the elders had called playtime. It was time to wash and dine and time for study hall and bed, and yet the rain continued to fall steadily and it wasn't even the rainy season yet!

7 • FAIRY DUST DEMONSTRATION

Lilly woke to the sound of rain still tapping against the windowpane? *Had it rained all night* she wondered? The chatter in the dorm was not as chipper as usual; no doubt the weather had something to do with that, she thought as she stretched in her warm, cozy bed.

Madame Louise opened the curtains, kissed each and every fairy on the forehead, and pointed each one of them toward the bathing room. They knew exactly what to do, no need to be told twice. As Madame made the rounds, Lilly was sure she didn't look quite right, but she didn't know why. Her hair was the same, her tunic was the same, and her smile was the same . . . or was it? Was it possible that Madame Louise was worried about something? What could she possibly be worried about? Lilly wasn't sure, but continued to read the unusual look on Madame's face as best she could.

"Lilly, dear, is something wrong?" Madame Louise asked softly pulling back Lilly's sheets.

Madame's question took Lilly by surprise; after all she was wondering the very same thing about Madame. Lilly assured Madame that all was well and rushed toward the bathing room before being questioned further. Madame Louise had taken her off guard; she was unprepared- very un-Lilly like indeed.

Pearle was perched upon the sink brushing out her beautiful hair. She was smiling, as usual, and asked Lilly if she would like a ride back to the dorm. Lilly tickled the back of little Pearle's neck as she walked past her.

"Why thank you Pearle," she said, "but I am running behind. You run along or we'll certainly both be late and we'll have tardy notes in hand before we know it!" Lilly stretched out her arms toward Pearle. "May I?" she asked.

Pearle didn't answer; she simply dove straight into Lilly's arms. Lilly proceeded to swing her around three times and one more for luck, before setting her gently down into her waiting chariot. Spinning around, Pearle tapped her lap for any potential riders, at which Rosie immediately dove on top of Pearle's tiny lap, and Ivy took up the rear. Off they all went, not an unusual site for first thing in the morning, though if one wasn't used to it, it did look quite odd. Three little fairies clanging through the dorm, giggling and laughing, with dripping hair and rosy cheeks and trying very hard not to run over the toes of their friends, as they rolled through the halls in Pearle's little chariot.

Lilly had cleaned her teeth, washed her face, and brushed her long golden curls. Her first lesson of the day was Task and Deeds. She liked her Task and Deeds lessons, especially after spending so much time in the dust factory. Lilly picked a lovely pressed pink dress from her wardrobe and slipped it on. She was just about to leave the dorm when she stopped, turned, and ran back toward her bed. There on the nightstand, where it always stood, was her beautiful little silver scoop, with her name inscribed on the side, the one that the foreman had personally given her. She picked it up, polished it on her dress, and slipped it into her pocket. Tasks and Deeds meant dust, fairy dust! All dust needed to be measured precisely according to the request, and Lilly had learned, as had Boris, that precise meant just that, not close to or close enough but exactly the amount requested and approved by the task manager. Not a grain more or less – precise meant just that! She would need her scoop and proudly tapped it in her pocket to be sure it was still there. Lilly was certain that even Boris had remembered his scoop for this lesson. She took one last look around the dorm and headed to the class-shroom.

Though Mademoiselle Francesca was Lilly's favorite elder, Mademoiselle Henrietta taught the Task and Deeds lesson. She was a lovely teacher, though her style and mannerisms were very different than those of Mademoiselle Francesca, who Lilly so admired.

"Today I shall require the assistance of Boris and Lilly," Mademoiselle Henrietta stated as soon as the class began. Everyone separated and allowed Lilly and Boris to walk to the front of the class.

Boris's eyes grew huge. He had no idea that he would be called upon, and he scanned Lilly's face to see if she was as surprised as he. It was clear that she was. Though Lilly was always happy to help, Boris was nervous to do so. To be in front of the class was not his cup of tea at all, and he wished he had Lilly's confidence, especially since all eyes were upon him!

"Boris, come up here dear, and please bring your scoop with you," Mademoiselle said. She waited patiently for him to stand by her side before continuing. "Boris if you could demonstrate dear how we should not, I repeat should not, dear, dip into the dust barrel. I think that would be a fabulous demonstration for you . . . do you mind showing the class the incorrect way to dip the dust?"

Boris didn't mind at all, he could demonstrate with ease the incorrect way to scoop dust. He made a mental note to himself to work on that personally, since that likely wasn't a good thing. Boris made a *B-line* straight toward the massive barrel of dust.

Mademoiselle removed the lid. The dust sparkled and danced, and in such a huge quantity it was always breathtaking. Mademoiselle Henrietta noticed how each little fairling was in awe at the very sight, and she couldn't help but smile. She, too, remembered as a small fairling, how each and every time she saw the dust in the large barrels, it took her breath away, although she didn't say so, it still did!

Boris pulled out his scoop and raised it into the air for everyone to see. Turning on his heels, he dug his scoop deep into the barrel as everyone watched to see what he would do next. Pulling the scoop out of the barrel, Boris held it once again for all to see; it was overflowing, dust spilling everywhere, though Boris purposely held the beautiful silver scoop over the barrel so not a single particle would be lost or wasted.

"This is how one *does not* dip into the barrel or measure the dust!" Boris said firmly, as he spun around slowly showing his classmates the scoop. "Note the waste, as it spills over the scoop and into the tub, that's exactly what a fairling should not do!"

Jack burst out laughing, at which Mademoiselle awarded demerits immediately. After all, she was very proud that Boris had taken his task so seriously. Jack accepted his d-merit slip, though he was having a terrible time believing Boris actually was up there demonstrating in the first place and so seriously at that! The look on Boris's face practically brought Jack to tears. Desperately, Jack tried to stop laughing; he didn't need any more demerits and was certain Madame had more on the way! He bit the inside of his own cheek it hurt, but it did help stop the laughing if only for a moment!

"Thank you, dear," Mademoiselle Henrietta said. "That

was a perfect demonstration!" She smiled and turned toward Lilly. "Lilly, we're ready for you dear."

Lilly strolled to the barrel, pulled out her scoop, and held it high above her head for everyone to see, just as Boris had. She pretended to check a chart for a task to verify how much dust would actually be required. She put a portion of dust into her scoop, took it to the balance scale, poured the excess back into the tiny silver scoop, and poured it back into the dust barrel. Lilly tapped her silver scoop gently on the side of the large barrel, ensuring all of the excess dust fell back into the tub. The whole class, including Mademoiselle Henrietta, applauded Lilly's perfect demonstration as not a single speck of fairy dust was wasted!

"Well," said Mademoiselle, "I believe our fabulous volunteers have demonstrated clearly what we should and should not do, in regards to measuring the exact amount of fairy dust for any task or deed you may be assigned." She looked at the faces of the fairies listening to her. "Are there any questions little ones?" But there were none. Hovering a perfect two inches off the ground, she instructed everyone to form a line at the rear of the dusting parlor, said her goodbyes, and then she simply disappeared.

"That was perfect, Lilly," Pearle whispered. "Now let's eat, I'm starving!"

Standing in line, staring at the choices, Boris couldn't decide between the fairy pot roast and battered fairy sandwiches, both were very good in their own right. It was Jack that made the decision for him, though Boris was actually quite pleased with Jack's choice.

"No pot roast today Boris," Jack said quite serious. "I'm certain the rain will let up and we will have a match, a Fairy Kick-a-Berry match, and pot roast is too heavy!"

Boris's eyes lit up. He loved Fairy Kick-a-Berry; it was his favorite game. He was very good at his position for which he was very proud, indeed, since he had earned the reputation for being one of the best defenders in the patch. He nudged Jack, smiled, and asked, "Are Lilly, Rosie, and Ivy playing with us today?"

Jack thought about the question; it was a serious one. Lilly, Rosie, and Ivy didn't usually play Fairy Kick-a-Berry, unless the match was specifically played for fun. Today was supposed to be a planned serious match, a competition of sorts; Jack had handpicked the team himself.

"Let's wait and see what they do," Jack said to Boris. "I don't think Jasper will pick the girls, but if Jasper picks

Nadine, Violet, and Sophie, then we shall pick Ivy . . . because she is very good at Fairy Kick-a-Berry." Ivy was very good and aggressive, though always at the appropriate times. "We shall also pick Rosie, of course." Jack hesitated, rolled his eyes and sat down at the dining table. Boris could clearly see he was trying to say something but didn't want to.

"Yes," Boris said, "say it, I know you're going to say it Jack . . . you have to!"

"Ahhhhhhhh, and we'll have to pick Lilly!" Jack finally blurted out, though he wasn't very happy about this pick at all. It was a necessary pick, so her feelings wouldn't be hurt. But Jack wasn't happy about it, not one little bit, and he liked Lilly, just not in a serious match of Fairy Kick-a-Berry!

He looked Boris straight in the eye and said, "Boris, if Lilly stops and straightens the ruffles on her dress even once, once Boris during play, well I'm telling you, I shall certainly lose my fairy mind much like Delyn in *Crazed Fairling on the Loose!*" He sounded quite serious, especially when he added, "Boris, for the good of the team, you shall have to talk to her!"

Boris couldn't help but wonder why, why it would have

to be him. Jack answered the question before Boris actually had a chance to ask it.

"She'll listen to you Boris without getting upset I mean," he said. "You know she'll listen and won't be sad. Just tell her to kindly leave her ruffles and the dust on her dress alone until after the match . . . tell her it's distracting and that we need her to focus . . . you'll think of something," Jack said this as Boris stared at him, mouth open, and eyes huge, as he pictured the look on Lilly's face when he tried to tell her such things!

Boris was not convinced that Jack's statement was true and that Lilly wouldn't be upset with him, but he would handle the task, and besides he was hoping to get lucky. Maybe Jasper wouldn't ask Nadine, Violet, or Sophie to play, and then he wouldn't have to talk to Lilly at all! Boris finished his meal and put it out of his mind, until they walked onto the soggy, water-covered kick a berry pitch and saw Jasper and his team, Nadine, Violet, and Sophie. His heart sank. He would have to say something to Lilly; there was no avoiding it!

Jack waived Ivy onto the pitch. She splashed water everywhere running full speed toward them. Rosie waited for her cue and walked toward them accordingly. Jack nudged Boris and reminded him to have gentle words with Lilly, as she came skipping onto the pitch jumping puddles every now and then along the way. To Lilly's credit, she was not offended at all when Boris asked very nicely if she wouldn't mind leaving the ruffles and the fairy dust on her dress alone until after the game, assuring her it was only until after the game. Boris turned and pointed toward Jack. "Jack would really appreciate it, as team captain of course, if you could focus on the match instead of your ruffles, if you don't mind of course."

Lilly thought it was the ideal time to let Boris off the hook. She smiled, curtseyed, and ran toward Pearle and the rest of the team.

Pearle blew the whistle. "May I have the team captains please?" As they approached she said, "Clean match everyone, clean match!"

Jasper and Jack walked to the half line and stood on either side of Pearle, they shook each other's hands.

"Clean match," they said in unison.

Pearle glanced at Jack and then at Jasper. "Okay, so we are clear on the rules?" she said. "Regular Fairy Kick a Berry rules will apply: no hovering, flying, disappearing, or reappearing down the pitch, and of course no hands!" She raised the whistle. "Any questions?" There were none. "Okay then," she said, "let the match begin," and she blew the whistle as loudly as she possibly could.

Jack took off with the kick-a-berry and flew toward the goal. He passed it to Sander, who passed the berry to Dante. Dante took the berry down the pitch, and then passed it back to Jack, who passed it to Ivy. Ivy dribbled around Lilly, because much to Ivy's despair, Lilly was splashing and jumping in the newly formed puddles that were on the pitch, even after she said she wouldn't! Jack was very appreciative of the move that Ivy had made, and even told her so. Ivy passed the ball to Jack. Jack dribbled all the way to the goal and scored!

Pearle was very excited, even popping a wheelie in her chair as she splashed through the water and rolled back to the half line, which was hardly visible. The rain had not stopped, but Lilly wondered if they should really be playing at all. After all, the pitch was covered with water and you could barely see the lines. Lilly was certain that her dress would never be the same, and her hair; well, her curls would have to be rewrapped for sure!

The berry headed toward Boris, but he was ready! He kept his eyes on it and the approaching player. Wiping the raindrops from his face, he focused on taking the berry from the opposing team. His opportunity had come, a slip in the water by his opposing teammate. He moved in, took the berry with ease, and with a swift, hard kick sent the kick-a-berry berry back up the pitch toward Jack.

Jack raced the berry toward the goal, as his opponent stepped in front of him, but Jack was ready. His eyes had already scoped out the opening positions, and Lilly, much to his dismay, was open. He yelled to her, and to his surprise though he was certain it was an accident, she not only listened but also dodged around an opposing player who had spotted the play. The berry was already in motion toward Lilly when she kicked the berry as hard as she possibly could. It flew through the air, impressing even Jack! It was about to miss, but Jack headed the berry into the goalmouth and between the two of them; Jack and Lilly scored the goal that secured the game! The rain had started to fall even heavier than before, it was absolutely pouring, and against everyone's will, except for Lilly's; it was time to stop the match.

Sander approached Pearle. "I have a request," he said.

"Speak," she giggled, "I do love this position!"

"If Jack agrees, I would like a rematch, when the

weather is fitting and the pitch is dry."

Pearle glanced at Jack, who answered for the team.

"Absolutely, we're in!" Jack said.

Jack ran toward Lilly, as did Boris, Rosie, Ivy, and Pearle. Grabbing her, they swung her around in the air. Lilly was very proud of herself though she didn't dare say, but Jack did and so did Boris, although Boris felt a tad guilty for mentioning the ruffles on her dress at all.

"We couldn't have done it without you, Lilly," Jack giggled. "I can't believe I just said that, no offense!"

There was none taken, given the circumstances of the soggy pitch and all; it had been an amazing game! Now they were all ready to dry out and warm up. Fairy cocoa would do the trick, with a lovely piece of chocolate fairy delight cake to take the edge off their newfound hunger. They ran back to the dorm to change out of their soaking wet clothes, met in the dining hall, and sipped their hot cocoa. They discussed every single detail of the kick-a-berry game that they had just played; there were many things that they had done right.

"Great goal, Lilly," Jack said.

"But you scored," Lilly replied. "I was the um, what do you call it Boris? I know . . . the assist!"

Jack smiled at Lilly. "No Lilly, you were the goal! Without you I couldn't have assisted you in scoring that fantastic goal!"

Lilly thought about that for a moment but was certain that Jack was just being nice. Either way, she'd had a fabulous time and Fairy Kick-a-Berry was not too bad. Though one thing was for sure – next time she most certainly could do without the rain!

8 • DISASTER AT HAND

Though not yet the rainy season, the rain fell as if it were. It had been raining nonstop for days. Flight 101 had been postponed until further notice, due to the landing area being completely underwater! Creative language arts had been cancelled due to the leaky roof of the shroom, and since the water was running through the colony so forcefully, there was no chance of leaf rafting anytime soon. On top of all of that, Lilly was certain the elders were gathering, but she had no idea why. It was actually Boris that confirmed Lilly's thoughts, as he sat down next to her in the study hall.

"Monsieur Claude is acting very strange," he said. "He keeps looking out the window and checking his pocket watch, as if he's expecting someone." Boris opened up a scroll and started to read. "You don't know if we're expecting anyone at the patch, do you Lilly?" he asked.

Lilly hadn't heard a thing about a visitor, but now she was very curious as to why the elders were acting so oddly. Glancing around the study hall, she noticed there wasn't an elder to be seen, very strange indeed. Lilly nudged Boris as he, too, looked around, agreeing that this was highly unusual, no elder in the study hall . . . why that was unheard of!

Jack sat down at the table with Lilly and Boris. He could tell Lilly had something on her mind.

"Yes?" he said staring at her.

"I didn't say anything," giggled Lilly.

"But you're going to," Jack said as he picked up Lilly's scroll.

Lilly wondered how Jack knew that she wanted to tell him that she thought something wasn't quite right. Momentarily getting lost in her thoughts, Jack brought her back to reality by snapping his fingers and saying, "Um, um."

"Lilly, what do you think is going on?" he asked.

Well she didn't know, and for the first time in a long

time Lilly didn't have a theory and told Jack so. Jack had heard from Sander that another shroom was leaking, and that they may all have more time on their hands before long. Maybe that's what it was, leaky shrooms!

"I hope it dries out soon," Jack whined, "so we can get on with our match or our rematch I should say!" He put his head down on the table. "I think I'm quite sick of all this rain, sick of it!"

Lilly wasn't in any hurry to play the next match. It really wasn't her cup of tea and yet she was committed to the rematch. She decided to turn the conversation back to the issue at hand, because she was certain that there was something wrong – she could sense it.

"May I have your attention please, your attention, dears, if you don't mind!" said the elder that suddenly appeared in front of the study hall.

Lilly recognized the voice immediately, it was Mademoiselle Francesca, and everyone turned and looked at her, giving her their undivided attention.

"It appears the rain is causing quite a problem. It seems as if the rainy season has come upon us a bit earlier than usual, and, well quite frankly, we're not prepared. The engineers have been summoned, including the Chief and

Master Engineers who are collaborating, accordingly, regarding the issues and problems that the rain seems to be posing." She took a deep breath, "We do not want you to be alarmed, though your lessons will likely be interrupted."

Boris turned to Lilly, who turned to Jack and then back to Boris. She had known it, there was something wrong, but what they didn't know was the magnitude of the problem, as Mademoiselle Francesca continued.

"We are asking that all lower class fairlings pay attention please. Once again, this announcement is for our lower class fairlings; upper class fairlings, your announcement will follow shortly."

Mademoiselle had the attention of every fairy, including Jack. "Lessons have been suspended until further notice." And that's when she lost Jack, as he leapt out of his chair with joy and hovered in the air two feet off the ground, until Lilly grabbed the tip of his foot and yanked him back down. Though Lilly never spoke, her scowl indicated that suspended lessons likely weren't a good thing . . . unless you were Jack!

Mademoiselle Francesca continued, "You will be under the supervision of your dorm monitors, their assistants, and the upper class fairlings, so with all due respect, behave . . .

that, Jack, means you!"

Boris nudged Jack as he tried desperately not to burst out laughing; he had thought that this was very funny, even Lilly had thought that it was funny, though inappropriate. Mademoiselle was not quite done.

"Don't be alarmed," she said. "There will be many Engineers and Master Engineers coming to and from the colony; some you will recognize and some you will not!"

Lilly's eyes grew huge – that news couldn't be good. Boris had no idea why visitors would be summoned, so he shrugged his shoulders and pointed to Jack, but Jack didn't have any idea either as to why outside Master Engineers would be brought to the patch.

"It is a precautionary measure only," Mademoiselle Francesca said noticing the buzz that had just started. "Your dorm monitors and upper class fairlings have assignments and activities to keep you busy. Just please bare with us. Hopefully the rain will end soon, the patch will dry out, and the engineers can make the necessary repairs." She was done, the fairlings had more than enough information, and besides she was ready for some rose hip tea, she was feeling quite parched.

It was Jack who spoke first. "Well Lilly, there you have

it . . . the mystery. There is a problem, and we do have visitors."

Boris nodded, Master Engineers, visiting Master Engineers, rain, suspended classes, there couldn't possibly be much more. Lilly, however, couldn't help but wonder why on earth leaky roofs would cause the elders to bring in outside help; surely there had to be more, another piece to the mystery. She decided to watch and listen very closely to everything that went on around her, and asked Boris and even Jack to do the same. Jack's observations, well they could be questionable, Lilly thought, since he was so often easily distracted, but Boris might pick up on a few interesting things. Maybe between the two of them, they could figure out what was really going on, or at least have fun trying.

"I do love a mystery," said Lilly. "Let's see if we can figure it out before they announce it."

Even Jack wanted to try to figure it out. "Can I be like a super secretive fairy agent, like agent 121?" he asked, "and I could wear a disguise."

Boris laughed, imagining Jack sneaking through the patch and knowing everyone would know it was Jack. "Jack, if you wear a disguise you will draw attention to yourself . . . not very spy like at all."

"Focus Jack, focus," Lilly said softly. "I really think that eyes and ears will suffice don't you?"

"You're right Lilly, no need to get your ruffles in a twist, no spy gear," Jack chuckled.

As soon as Jack told Lilly not to get her ruffles in a twist, it was over. Boris was laughing so hard that there would be no reasoning with him or Jack anytime soon. Lilly could tell that Boris was trying to apologize, but he was laughing so hard he simply couldn't. It was almost funny, almost, but quite frankly, she'd had enough of the both of them. Putting her scrolls into her satchel, she said good-bye and waltzed off to the dining hall, tossing the ruffles on her pink dress as she did so!

Lilly caught her first glimpse of the elders and the Master Engineers, including the guests, from the window in the dining hall. They were standing in the rain gathered under a large mushroom. The Master Engineer appeared to be discussing something quite serious, pointing and saying something as the others poked at the mushroom. He stared down at his scroll while talking with the elders. He was tall by any pixie standard, and he looked well aged, even for an elder. His eyes were very small, and she could tell that he was very serious about whatever it was they were discussing. His safety helmet was the whitest white that Lilly had ever seen, as was his coat. For a moment she thought he was the safety inspector from the factory then realized that he wasn't.

He held blue scrolls in his hands and referred back to them often during the course of his conversation. The Chief Engineer appeared to have questions, and the Master looked as if he were pointing to the stem of the mushroom they were standing under and then back at the scrolls simultaneously. Though Lilly couldn't imagine why, she continued to watch and was slightly startled when Pearle rolled up beside her to take a peek as well. Lilly thought that the Master Engineer had on a pair of spectacles but couldn't be certain due to the distance, and with the rain that was rolling down the windowpane, it was difficult to tell.

"As you can see Chief, we have a problem," the Master Engineer said passing the scroll to the Chief.

"I'm afraid you're right. How bad do you believe it is?" the Chief asked examining the scroll.

Everyone held their breaths to see what the Master Engineer would say, but he didn't answer immediately, he checked his calculations one more time to be certain. The Master Engineer took off his helmet and scratched his head then took a deep breath and proceeded to speak.

"Well I'm certain we can all agree that upon first examination all appears well, but unfortunately that is not the case!"

Monsieur Claude placed an arm around Mademoiselle Francesca, Mademoiselle Francesca grasped Madame Louise's hand, and Madame Louise grabbed Monsieur Pierre's hand. The Chief motioned for the Engineer to continue, which he did, though he chose his words very carefully.

"First and foremost, let me say that there's still hope. We can salvage the situation, though it will require, no doubt, the entire effort of the colony!"

Everyone gasped, how bad could it be?

"Not to worry," the Master Engineer said recognizing the worry on the elders' faces. "I really think we can handle this, though we shall have to work diligently through the night, I am sure." He pointed to the stalk of the mushroom as he spoke. "As you know, each year prior to the rainy season, we treat the colony for rot, mushroom rot to be exact."

Everyone nodded and the Master Engineer continued.

"This season, two things have happened that have created a very serious situation for the mushroom patch indeed!" He took a deep breath and switched scrolls, adjusted his spectacles, and continued. "Normally pre-rain season, we treat all of the mushrooms, every one of them, with the mushroom rot protective coating. We spray them from top to bottom, inside and out." He paused to make sure that he still had a captive audience and he did, so he continued. "This coating seals and hardens on the mushrooms, keeps the water out, and keeps the structure strong and sturdy, as it should be, while preventing mold, rot, and damage." Everyone was still listening.

"Due to the early rain season, one: the formula was not applied, but it wouldn't have mattered anyway since it wasn't available yet; and two: and this one is hard for me to say, but more importantly, due to an early rain season, the moisture has taken its toll!" He took off his spectacles, pushed his helmet onto the back of his head and continued, "We have weak stalks, but even worse than that . . . I know," he said shaking his head as he read the fear on the elders' faces. "Yes, I'm afraid that what you are thinking is correct. We have rot, mushroom rot in the mushroom patch!"

Everyone gasped at the very same time, and then it went silent for what seemed like several minutes, but was actually only moments.

"This is disastrous!" the Chief said. "What will we do? If it doesn't stop raining, the rot will get worse, and it will spread from shroom to shroom. We will lose our colony, our homes, our class-shrooms, our infirmary, and what if someone becomes ill, oh this is disastrous! Mushroom rot in the mushroom patch, why I never thought I'd see the day!"

The Master Engineer raised his hands, trying his best to calm the elders before the panic set in. "Allow me to continue," he said.

"Just listen for a few more moments. Everything will be fine. I have a plan and in fact, it's already in motion!"

9 • TEAMWORK

Lilly and Pearle could see the serious nature of the conversation but had no idea what it was about; they continued to watch from the dining hall window. Pearle knew Lilly was concerned, and although Pearle had no idea what it could possibly be, she was certain Lilly would figure it out!

"Lilly what do you think is wrong?" Pearle asked. "Why do they keep poking the mushroom?"

Lilly's eyes grew huge. Pearle may have just figured it out! "I think that's it dear Pearle," she said. "I think you figured it out. The mushrooms, there's something wrong with the mushrooms but what – what could it possibly be?"

Mademoiselle Francesca asked if the mixture were

available yet, and if so, could they apply it right then. The Master Engineer tried to explain.

"I'm afraid, dear Mademoiselle that applying the mixture right now, in the condition that the mushrooms are in, would not actually do any good. Essentially, we would be wasting the mixture and not helping the shrooms." He could tell that she needed a little more information, so he proceeded with his explanation. "You see, when we typically apply the coating, the mushrooms are dry, bone dry. The coating goes onto the mushroom, the first layer soaks in, the second sticks on top and does just that; it coats the mushrooms. It seals and hardens them to the touch, the sturdy, strong texture you're used to." He took her hand and put it on the stem of the mushroom that they were standing under. "Go ahead, give it a push, a squeeze if you will; it's too soft, the damage is done!"

Mademoiselle pushed the stem of the mushroom, and it wobbled to her touch. It was squishy and soft, and not the shrooms that they were used to at all. "What to do, what will we do?" she asked softly, trying to hold back her own tears. "For even I know mushroom rot spreads like wild fire!"

The Chief and the other engineers looked at the Master

Engineer and the visiting Master Engineer for answers; the Master Engineer motioned toward the guest to take the floor.

"Well we do have a plan in motion, but I am hopeful that our outside guest will have additional insight, shall we say, regarding this potentially damaging situation!" said the Master Engineer as he prepared to introduce the visitor.

Everyone turned toward the guest Master Engineer. "This is Monsieur Jean Claude, Monsieur if you please," the Master Engineer said. "Please sir, anything you have to offer would be greatly appreciated. You know what I have already put in motion, and now the floor is yours."

All of the elders including the Master Engineer turned attentively to Monsieur Jean Claude and waited patiently for him to begin. He was slight in stature, with deep furrowed lines on his brow. His eyes were dark, almost black, and his nose was very pointed. But every elder knew that if the Master Engineer had summoned him, he knew something that their Engineer did not, and they were right.

Monsieur Jean Claude knew mushroom rot – it was his specialty, his area of expertise – and he knew that the mushroom rot, in the mushroom patch was a very rare form of the rot, indeed. However, he had seen it before!

He had been incredibly fortunate to study in foreign lands and knew exactly what needed to be done.

"Umm, umm," clearing his throat and walking toward the mushroom, Monsieur Jean Claude began to explain his recommendation for eradicating the mushroom rot. "Do not worry, dear colony. It is as bad as you think, but not as bad as it could be, and this believe it or not is very good news indeed!"

Mademoiselle Francesca squeezed Madame Louise's hand. There was hope she could feel deep within and took a deep breath as she waited for Monsieur Jean Claude to continue.

"It is imperative, and I cannot stress this enough, imperative," he said for the second time, "that we destroy the rot already present on the shrooms that are damaged." He pointed to the stalk of the shroom they were standing under. Cutting off a piece of the top layer, he revealed a layer of rot, mushroom rot.

Everyone agreed that made perfect sense, but what were his recommendations? They couldn't possibly cut each mushroom up layer by layer searching for the rot; they waited to see what he would say. The guest Engineer flipped his scroll over, scribbled with his quill, and after reading his own note, he continued:

"We have to accomplish two things in order to eradicate the rot completely and keep it from spreading and destroying the entire colony. We must remove the rot from the shrooms that have it, burn the damaged tissue, and treat what's left. Then we must treat all the other mushrooms with the preventive mixture coating that we always use for pre-rain season. As you know, this will not be easy. Per the colony's Master Engineer's explanation, the mushrooms must be dry!" He paused and looked at the faces of his peers, studying them momentarily before continuing. "Now I am certain that you are wondering how we can accomplish such a task of this magnitude." Respectfully they continued to listen.

"The obviously damaged mushrooms, all of them, must go. If we are uncertain, an engineer will test, just like I did via a blade, cut the mushroom, and check the rot to diagnose. All of the damaged tissue will be burned in the pit, preventing the rot from spreading from mushroom to mushroom." The visiting Engineer took a breath, put down his scroll, and looked into the eye of each elder. "The second phase will be difficult, but manageable; it will require the assistance of everyone, and it is already in motion."

The elders were anxious, they had no idea what it could possibly be and no idea what to expect. Patiently they waited for him to continue.

"We have already assembled a crew. The factory shift workers that are currently off duty are right now, as we speak, deep in the forest searching for the big-eared plant, or plants I should say, who's leaves we will need, – and we will need many!"

The Master Engineer, Monsieur Jean Claude, turned to Mademoiselle Francesca. "If I may be so bold, could you assemble all of the seamstresses in the colony or anyone that can sew, at this time, please? I will find you and explain when it's time!"

Without even asking why, Mademoiselle Francesca simply said, "Consider it done," and disappeared and then reappeared to gather the seamstresses.

Monsieur continued, "The factory workers will be required at shift change to work in the dust factory, and though the crews are exhausted, it is imperative that the shift leaving the factory takes over the search for the big-eared plants." He looked sad as he spoke, "It truly is the only way, and who better to work via shift than our perfect factory workers?" Putting his head down, he added, "Though they are already tired from the long, hard hours in the factory, we must depend on them still!"

It was the Master Engineer that finally asked, "Monsieur, what will we do with the big-eared plants?"

"We will gather the leaves of the big-eared plant and use the colony fairy dust sparingly. Only when the leaves can no longer be stacked higher manually, then may the dust be applied. Do you agree?" Monsieur asked the elders. Naturally they all agreed. It was not a good time to go deep into the mines and using the dust sparingly was wise.

"We shall also use the dust for transport, simply because time is not on our side where the mushroom rot in the mushroom patch is concerned."

The plan was starting to become clear; they would gather the big-eared plant leaves, transport them from the forest to the colony and dry them just enough so that they were pliable, and so that the seamstresses could sew them together.

"Once the seamstresses have sewn the big-eared plant leaves together, we shall form canopies to protect the mushrooms from the rain, placing the big-eared plant leaves over the mushrooms so they may start to dry. Once they are dry, we will apply the mixture, the protective coating. The canopies will be suspended via the vine cables in the trees and branches that cover our patch. In the meantime, the engineers will destroy and burn the damaged mushrooms, so the mushroom rot does not spread." He took a deep breath. "But we must work quickly, since time is not on our side!" He took a sip of lilac tea and continued, "I'm sorry, dear elders, that there is no point or time for questions, because unfortunately we have no other solutions." He rolled up his scrolls and dismissed the crowd gathered around him.

Monsieur Claude mopped his brow. "I will gather my young fairlings, so they can provide water and fairy cress sandwiches to ensure the shift workers maintain their strength," he said. The Master Engineer smiled warmly, agreeing that was a wonderful, thoughtful, and a necessary plan.

"I know several fairlings such as Lilly, Pearle, Rosie, not necessarily Ivy, but others that can help the seamstresses sew, and I will gather them," said Madame Louise, as she turned on her heels and simply disappeared.

Everyone was working for the good of the colony, working together for a common goal. The colony was salvageable. The mushroom patch was buzzing. Excitement, fear, uncertainty, and all levels of emotions were running through the minds of each and every elder and fairy, particularly the young ones, but to their credit not one said a negative word. Even if they thought it, they never, ever voiced it.

Boris was uncertain of what he was supposed to do. He was trying to hand out glasses of water, but to his dismay all of his workers wanted tea, rose hip tea. He didn't have any tea, and though he would like to have some himself, he didn't have any to offer. Feeling quite disappointed that he didn't have any tea to offer the workers, Boris asked Jack if he could please stop kicking the berry for a minute, and see if Cook wouldn't mind putting the kettle on for a large pot of rose hip tea for the shift workers. They were, after all, wet, tired, and cold, and the tea would likely cheer them up as well as warm them. Jack kicked the berry into his hands, smiled, and disappeared. Boris looked around anxiously, scared to death that Jack would get caught, since fairlings were not cleared yet to disappear and reappear to speed up travel!

Lilly was so happy that Mademoiselle Francesca had needed her help, and on such an important matter too.

Rosie, Pearle, and Nadine all gathered the vine thread that they would be using. To Lilly's surprise, Ivy had volunteered though she didn't want to. She was irritated but didn't dare say a word. It was for such a worthy task that she couldn't possibly perform it with anything less than a happy heart; though her happy heart, had some much needed adjusting. Ivy handled the task nicely. She hated to sew, she was not very good at it, and fortunately they were not receiving a grade for their craftsmanship. Knowing Ivy would rather be cutting down big-eared plant leaves, Lilly offered her a different task, the task of actually cutting the stems off the leaves.

"There are scissors involved," Lilly said with a smile, "and I'm sure if you can't cut it properly, you could tear it!"

Ivy giggled at Lilly standing there, so delicate and pink! "Dear Lilly, you are so nice," she said. "Thank you! I would love to cut and tear, versus sew and iron the big-eared leaves. Hand me the scissors!"

The rain continued to fall, but the shift workers never stopped nor complained! They drudged through the mud and the newly formed streams that ran through the forest. Not daring to waste the dust, they endured the weather and the miserable conditions that the rain had left in its wake.

"Coming down, watch out below . . . watch out below!" said one of the shift workers hovering above the treetop. "Here's another one, and it's a biggie."

As the big-eared plant leaves tumbled to the ground, the factory workers stacked them as high as they possibly could. When they could no longer reach the top, they sprinkled the tiniest amount of dust on the pile. At that very moment, the pile rose up to them, suspended in midair until the task was complete, and then with a wave of the Master Engineer's wand, the entire pile disappeared and then reappeared in the middle of the mushroom patch.

Second shift workers took the pile and carried it into the dining hall, where all of the leaves were laid out to dry in front of the large hearths and the roaring fires. Once the leaves were almost dry, the seamstresses began their work, including Ivy.

Lilly was a beautiful seamstress in the making, though that surprised no one. She took great pride in everything she did, including sewing. Stitch by stitch, she sewed two sides of two separate leaves together, over and over, with beautiful, perfect stitches. Pearle worked to the other side of her, and Pearle, too, sewed beautifully. Glancing up, Lilly couldn't help but smile as Ivy butchered a leaf to pieces.

Obviously, she couldn't cut it, so the tearing process had begun. Ivy was in her glory ripping and tearing the leaf; her lilac dress had turned green! Lilly couldn't even begin to imagine that there was a wash-sud in the wash-shroom strong enough to remove such a stain.

The entire colony was at work, but not a single elder, fairling, pixie, or visitor complained. As the canopies became available, a crew appeared, took them, and disappeared and reappeared back at the mushroom patch. One by one the mushrooms were covered by canopies, suspended by vines and stakes – the engineers and architectonics had done a marvelous job. The drying process had begun, though the rain continued to fall. As soon as the mushrooms were dry, the scientists would spray each one with the seal. The mushroom rot that was in the mushroom patch would be more than contained; it would be eradicated!

The Master Engineer embraced Monsieur Jean Claude. He was so pleased and proud of the work that the colony had completed together; teamwork seemed like an understatement . . . it was family work, at its best!

"Today," said the Master Engineer, "marks a day in colony history, one for the books, I might add!" Lilly was certain she saw him wipe a tear from his eyes. "I am so proud of all of you, from our shift workers who never stopped to our beautiful little fairlings, who assisted without complaint. Together we have saved our mushrooms, our colony, where we live, learn, play, and our home . . . our home!" He couldn't finish his speech, but everyone knew what he was trying to say. They had all worked hard and worked together for the good of their colony, their mushroom patch, and their home.

Lilly wiped away her own tears, though she wasn't sad. Jack would not look up; though his foot never left his kick-a-berry berry. Boris nudged Jack, which indicated they were both touched and felt proud to have been a part of the moment too. Boris smeared a great big tear away with his sleeve that had rolled down his cheek, and Lilly handed him a lovely clean handkerchief, for which he was grateful. It had ended well; the patch would survive the mushroom rot. Mushroom rot in the mushroom patch had brought them all together in a way that Lilly didn't know was possible.

Mademoiselle put her arm around Lilly and Pearle, "I think it's time, Master Engineer, to tuck in the little ones," she said, and he agreed.

Lilly fell between her cool crisp sheets, for she, like the

others, was exhausted. For the first time, she was actually thrilled that the lessons had been cancelled. Though she would still rise early, she wouldn't have to think about her studies at this time. She glanced at the shiny silver scoop sitting next to her bed and smiled. Liam and the foreman had been so funny the day they rafted down the stream on the leaf. River leaf rafting – now that had been fun! Her mind drifted to the big-eared plants, Rosie and Ivy, Boris and Jack. Before she knew it, Lilly's mind quit racing and it just went blank, and Lilly fell fast asleep!

10 • KICK-A-BERRY

It was no surprise that every fairling in the colony was starving the next morning, Lilly included. They were serving fairy porridge with cooked daffy berries cooked throughout and golden treacle drizzled on top to complete the dish, a treat for sure.

"I love this daffy berry porridge," Boris giggled as he nudged Jack. "Ask Cook for extra treacle. I'll trade you!"

Cook never gave Boris extra treacle; his girth did not require such. But she often commented that Jack was too slight and needed to eat more; extra treacle, well that made Cook very pleased indeed. As they ate the porridge together, it was Jack who noticed something odd, a sound or lack of one.

"Hey listen, it's not raining," he said.

For the first time in what seemed like forever, the rain had come to an end. The closer they looked, they realized that the sun was poking through the clouds, good news for the drying process. Jack's eyes lit up. The kick-a-berry pitch would dry out soon, and then they could have their rematch. He ate his porridge with a smile on his face. After breakfast the fairlings gathered in the study hall. Jack had a kick-a-berry in hand, but Boris knocked it to the ground.

"Pass it?" he asked.

Jack didn't need to be asked twice, and to the nearest hallway they went only to return a few minutes later. Lilly, Rosie, Ivy, and Pearle were playing fairy-shrades with Nadine, Violet, and Sadie, and Lilly had the floor.

"Cook a something," shouted Pearle.

"Rolling, baking, cooking, oh, I have no idea, Lilly," giggled Rosie.

Jack finally said, "What does it sound like?"

Collapsing on the floor, Pearle dove into Lilly's lap. "My turn," she said. "I got it right!'

Jack motioned to Lilly. "Can I have a word, Lilly, please," he asked bashfully. Lilly excused herself and joined Boris and Jack in the hallway, though as soon as she saw the kick-a-berry berry, she turned on her heels and walked away. Boris gently grabbed her arm and asked her to stay since Jack wanted to talk to her, so reluctantly she did. Jack opened his mouth to talk but closed it again. He tried again but couldn't seem to form the words that he wanted to say. He shook his head and glanced at Boris pleading, with his eyes for help, though he never asked for help, and Boris knew Jack was having difficulty explaining to Lilly what he had in mind.

Boris rolled the kick-a-berry toward Lilly; it landed right at the tip of her shoes. Very softly he mumbled the words, "We were just wondering if you wanted to practice, I mean play, if you wanted to play, practice, no I mean play, dribbling kick-a-berry skills in the hallway."

Jack shook his head. Boris had actually said it worse than he could have, though Jack knew Boris didn't mean to. Boris realized it wasn't quite coming out the way he and Jack had practiced the conversation that they had hoped to have with Lilly. He got nervous, threw up his hands and stared at Jack for help.

Lilly was quite amused, they were both very uncomfortable, indeed, and she thought now would be a really great time to let them off the hook, so she picked up the berry.

"Jack," she said, "Would you feel better if I practiced kick-a-berry skills with you?"

Jack's eyes lit up. He would feel much better and was very grateful that Lilly had understood. "If it's not too much trouble, Lilly, Boris and I thought we could help brush up on our skills and show you some new ones . . . if you have time, of course."

Lilly was impressed. Jack and Boris had asked so nicely. After all, she didn't know how she could possibly refuse them. Taking the berry with her, she walked to the far end of the hallway. She reminded the boys that there usually wasn't any kick-a-berry played indoors, but she thought under the circumstances, it would go unnoticed.

Jack nudged Boris. "Thanks mate," he whispered, "Jasper will have his hands full with us!"

Lilly placed the kick-a-berry berry at her feet, and her tiny hands straightened the wrinkle that had formed on her dress. Boris glanced at Jack, but Jack didn't flinch. She took a deep breath, swung her leg, and kicked the berry toward Jack. It didn't roll toward him very quickly, and it was noticeably crooked. Boris was certain that Jack was going to correct Lilly, but he didn't; he simply stopped the berry with his foot and kicked it back. Two things happened when Jack did this: one, Lilly watched very closely, for she was paying attention, and two: when the berry rolled back toward her and she returned it, she copied what Jack had just done exactly.

Lilly stopped the berry with her foot and Boris was so impressed he turned and gave Jack a quick thumbs up! She rolled the berry with her foot and centered it in the middle of the hallway. Taking two steps back, Lilly ran toward the berry and Boris was stunned. Lilly running in the hallway was unheard of! Her leg made contact with the berry, and it rolled toward Jack perfectly straight and with speed.

"Nice one, Lilly!" shouted Jack, and Boris agreed. "Do it again," Jack said, passing the berry back toward her.

Lilly passed the berry perfectly several times and suddenly had an audience; even Ivy was impressed. Stopping only once to admire the sparkling dancing dust on her dress, Lilly focused on the drill at hand. Jack passed the berry to her again as Boris appeared in front of Lilly, and Jack wondered what Lilly would do. He had no idea whether she would freeze or move around Boris. Lilly had never seen such a serious look on Boris's face before. She kicked the berry between Boris's legs, and Boris was momentarily stunned. He had no idea Lilly would think of such an amazing move, especially without any sideline instruction from Jack or the others.

"Lilly, that was wonderful," Boris said hoping he had hid the surprise he had felt. "I think she's ready Jack, don't you?"

To her surprise, Lilly was quite enjoying herself. Kick-a-berry was turning out to be quite fun, even in the hallway. Jack applauded Lilly for applying critical thinking and outmaneuvering Boris, which was not easy to do during a kick-a-berry game. Jack grabbed the berry as it rolled toward to him, scooped it up, and walked toward Lilly.

"Lilly thank you for practicing with me and Boris," he said. "I know that wasn't your favorite thing to do, but we appreciate your efforts."

Lilly was touched that Jack had been so nice about the skills practice, and she assured him that between then and the rematch, the kick-a-berry berry would become her new best friend, and she wasn't kidding. For the next several days, while everything dried out, Lilly had a berry in her hands or at her feet. She dribbled it as best she could and carried it under her arm. If there was no room to dribble it, she passed it between Ivy, Rosie, Boris, and Jack. She was quite enjoying it, really. They were in the midst of passing the berry back and forth when Pearle noticed something out of the corner of her eye. Swinging around in her chariot, she made her way to the window and peered out.

"Oh my, they're bringing down the canopies," she said pressing her nose even closer to the windowpane. "Ah, and now the lead scientists are spraying the mushrooms with what must be the sealant." She turned and looked at Lilly. "You know I've never really paid attention to that before, have you?"

Lilly hadn't noticed, but neither had the others. The elders always took care of everything, and the fairlings knew if something were happening in the patch, well, there was a reason for it. They all realized for the first time how hard the elders worked to protect their colony, though, despite their efforts, some things were beyond their control. They hadn't given that much thought to mushroom rot in the mushroom patch before, until it had threatened their home. It was something Lilly was certain that they would not take for granted anymore, their homes or how precious the mushroom patch actually was. Jack was thinking the very same thing.

"I can't believe that we could have lost our homes, and

I shudder at the thought. In fact I'm going to put it out of my mind," he said shaking his head as if to get the thoughts from his head.

"Well, I have an idea," said Boris.

Everyone waited to see what he would say, and he didn't disappoint.

"Let's go to the pitch and see if it's dry. If it is, we'll practice for the match, and if it's not, then at least we'll have an idea how many more moons we have to sleep through until it is!"

They played leap a fairy all the way. The ruffles from Lilly's dress were the only thing anyone could see each time she leapt over Jack's back. Jack purposely knocked Boris to the ground, but Boris didn't seem to mind. Ivy ran on ahead, desperate to see the condition of the pitch, with Rosie skipping behind all of them.

"Smashing," shouted Boris. "Look Jack, it's almost dry. I bet by this time tomorrow we can play the rematch!"

Lilly's heart raced, and she suddenly felt very anxious. Knowing that the match was coming and having it upon her were two totally different things. She turned incredibly pale, so much so that she plopped down on the ground right where she stood. Ivy, Rosie, Boris, and Jack burst out in giggles, while assuring her all would be well. Lilly was not convinced, though managed a half-hearted smile as she pulled herself to her feet.

"I think I may actually toss my fairy delights!" she said very bluntly. "Yep, I may actually pull a Boris . . . no offense Boris!'

Slowly they walked back to the mushroom patch, assuring Lilly that all would be fine as soon as she sipped on ginger lemon tea. Rosie ran on ahead to ensure that Cook would put the kettle on. Even Lilly wished she were able to at least hover back, but wouldn't dream of it since Mademoiselle had not cleared her to do so.

"Don't worry Jack, I can do this," Lilly assured him.

Jack never doubted she could, since she had put her mind to it and she had worked so hard practicing. He didn't say a word; he just put an arm around her shoulder and rubbed the curls right out of her hair! A sure sign that Jack is happy thought Lilly. Though she knew those curls were going to have to be rewrapped, she didn't breathe a word!

11 • THE MATCH

The day had finally arrived for the kick-a-berry rematch! Lilly opened her eyes but didn't have the nerve to climb out of bed. Her stomach was dancing; it was in knots inside of her, and for the first time since she had run through the forest to find help for Boris, she couldn't breathe, or at least felt as if she couldn't.

"My heart is racing, I just know it," she said out loud, though not a soul was around to hear her complaint. It was for the best, because it was certainly very un-Lilly like to complain at all, and she was surprised and disappointed in herself for doing so. Though she didn't want to, Lilly sat up in bed. She pulled her sheets up around her chin and pulled her knees close to her chest, but she was still convinced that she couldn't breathe. For a split second she contemplated going to the infirmary. Surely she was ill, she must be, since she felt absolutely awful. She checked her own pulse and even her own forehead, but it was no good – she was normal!

Lilly realized that Madame Louise must have allowed her to sleep in, since no other fairling was in the dorm. She must have been exhausted, she thought, to sleep so late at all. Reluctantly, she climbed out of bed and made her way toward the bathing room. She splashed cold water on her face and checked her forehead one more time just to be sure she wasn't ill . . . to her dismay, she was fine! Slowly she unraveled the cloth that wrapped her hair and long ringlets fell out one by one. It had never taken Lilly so long to get dressed. Brushing her hair, she purposely counted one hundred strokes, something typically saved for her evening routine. It was no use, she had to go to the match, because Jack was counting on her and so was Boris! She stood in front of her wardrobe, and her eyes scanned her lovely pink dresses. One dress had one ruffle and one had two. One dress was trimmed in white, one in dark pink, and one had lovely tiny pearls sewn in. Lilly became quite frustrated with herself and she told herself so, "Oh stop it,

Lilly, just pick a dress!"

She closed her eyes, extended her arm, and waited for her hand to get stuck on a hanging rod. As soon as it did, she pulled out the dress that accompanied it, only to put it back and purposely choose another. Lilly was quite embarrassed when Madame Louise appeared behind her, since she had no idea that she was even there. Although Lilly couldn't wait until she was able to do that, she didn't always like it when the elders disappeared and reappeared on a whim.

"Lilly, dear," Madame Louise said softly, "its almost time to go. The dresses are all lovely, just pick one."

Madame stepped behind Lilly, straightened the dress Lilly had chosen, tied the ribbon Lilly had placed in her hair, and held out her hand. "Shall we?" she asked.

As soon as Lilly's hand slipped into Madame's, the two disappeared and reappeared in the dining hall. Madame Louise looked down at little Lilly and smiled, assuring her that she would do a fabulous job, but, above all, she told Lilly to enjoy the match and have fun.

"It's a kick-a-berry match, and although it's important to play and try hard, it's just as important to have fun and enjoy being with the team, your new team, and one that you are now an important member of," Madame Louise said softly.

Lilly hadn't once thought about being part of a team, any team, let alone a kick-a-berry team. But all of a sudden, she supposed she was. She felt quite proud really, and Madame had been right; she should enjoy this new adventure. Lilly took a deep breath and decided right there and then that the kick-a-berry match, with her new team, was simply a new adventure, one that she hoped to conquer of course, but an adventure none the less. Her mood about the entire thing had suddenly changed for the better!

"Oh thank goodness, Lilly, there you are!" cried Jack. He was so relieved to see her that he really did almost cry. "I thought for certain that you had changed your mind, but I'm very happy you didn't!"

"Did you find her?" Boris asked.

Lilly knew that voice and she knew it well. She looked at Jack. "I've got this one, Jack," she said. "I wasn't lost dear Boris, were you?"

Boris grabbed Lilly and hugged her so hard she could barely talk. "Okay, you can put me down now Boris . . . Boris, put the pink fairy down!"

Boris put Lilly down and proceeded to explain, one more time, the official kick-a-berry match rules. "They're very, very, very, important Lilly!" he said.

"Yes Boris, I understand . . . they're very important," she replied.

Boris was quite serious about the rules and with one look at his face, Lilly thought it might be a good time to let him continue. "I'm sorry, Boris, please go ahead and explain the rules, if you don't mind."

Boris took a deep breath and said the following: "Please, Lilly, pay attention. I don't mean that in a bad way, but look, Lilly – Lilly the ruffles, Lilly . . .!"

Lilly blushed and purposely put her hands behind her back. She tried to ignore that one speck she could see out of the corner of her eye, but as soon as Boris was through explaining the rules, that one speck of dust that was out of place would be gone for sure!

Boris continued:

"First and foremost, absolutely no hovering!"

"No hands!"

"No disappearing or reappearing down the field or midfield for that matter!"

"No fairling can move, until the whistle is blown!"

"Offside rules apply. Any questions, ask Jack . . . they still confuse me!"

"Absolutely no hands E V E R, ever Lilly, ever!"

"You may dribble and pass the berry of course . . . I just thought that I would remind you!"

"Always take a shot, if you think you can!"

"Stay out of the goalie box . . . unless I need help. If I am in the goal . . . I will make it very clear, if I need help that is!"

"You may jump over the berry during play. That's all right, isn't it Jack?"

It was, Jack confirmed.

"Anything else, Jack? Did I miss anything, anything at all?" Boris asked.

Lilly was certain Boris had covered everything and told him so, but if she didn't remove that speck from her ruffle, well she might just lose her mind. Just as soon as Boris gave her the okay to leave and warm up, Lilly removed the speck of dust that had planted itself on her dress! Finally she could relax. Now what was Boris saying, she asked herself . . . but then giggled, because, after all, she had heard every word!

Jasper walked to the half line with his team behind him:

Zeraz, Harold, Henri, Nadine, Sophie, and Violet. Jack joined them followed by Boris, Pierre, Sander, Ivy, Rosie, and last but not least, Lilly. Everyone looked very smart in kick-a-berry uniforms, and though Lilly had insisted on wearing the jersey over her dress, she still looked very smart too.

The official referee glanced at Jack and then at Jasper. "Gentle fairlings," he said, "your teams are aware of the official kick-a-berry rules?" Everyone nodded; they all knew the rules, including Lilly with thanks to Boris! "Fair enough then," the referee said, "take your positions on the pitch, please. It's time . . . *Fairy Kick-a-Berry, Game On*!"

The referee blew his whistle and dropped the kick-a-berry berry from his hands. Jasper managed to touch the berry first; it was his team's possession. Down the pitch he went, dribbling in and out of his opponents as they tried desperately to take the berry. Jack finally took the berry from Jasper, switched directions, and headed toward the goal.

Harold wasn't having it. "Not so fast," he said, stepping in front of Jack and kicking the berry as hard as he could. The berry flew into the air and landed in front of Boris and Nadine. Nadine was faster, so she took the berry, ran between Boris and Jack, passed to Henri, and moved toward the goal.

Lilly was very grateful that the berry was nowhere near her, though she had heard Jack on more than one occasion remind her to keep her eyes on the berry at all times. She was trying to, but there was a lovely patch of daisies by the side of the pitch, and she couldn't help but wonder how on earth they ended up, in of all places, right there!

"Focus, Lilly, for just a minute on the kick-a-berry match," she told herself, so there was no need for Boris to, but he did anyway, though nicely of course.

"Lilly, Lilly the berry, keep your eye on it!" Boris whispered as he rushed past her.

Lilly blushed. Boris had been right; she had been distracted but was focused now. Her eyes watched the berry move toward her, and her heart sank, as Sophie got closer. Desperately she hoped Jack was coming to assist, but she saw him midfield. Boris was at the centerline, Rosie at her side, and Ivy in goal. Lilly watched Sophie who was surrounded by players, and they were running full speed directly to her. Just when Lilly thought it couldn't possibly get any worse, it did. Instinctively her wings sped up, and Jack noticed this immediately.

"Lilly no," he yelled, "no flight!"

Then Jack noticed Lilly raising her tiny hands toward her face, and once again he called out as he saw the berry in midair.

"Lilly, no hands in kick-a-berry, no hands!" he yelled down the pitch.

Lilly watched as Sophie kicked the berry as hard as she could toward Violet, but Violet was behind Lilly. Lilly noticed the berry once again in midair starting to drop. Her tiny hands instinctively rose to push the berry away and shield her beautiful, delicate little face.

"No hands, Lilly," screamed Boris, unaware of how fast the berry was travelling.

With wings fluttering, feet barely on the ground, and hands about her face, Lilly clamped her eyes shut, turned her head, and put her tiny hands down. The berry slammed straight into Lilly's head and face. She fell straight backwards, as if knocked completely out. The match stopped play, and the crowd that had gathered grew silent.

Boris ran toward Lilly, as fast as his legs could carry him, and though he knew he shouldn't, Jack hovered right above her. Lilly slowly sat up a little dazed, but she sat up.

"I didn't touch the berry," she cried. "No hands!"

Jack helped Lilly to her feet. She thanked him, and straightened her grass-stained ruffles on her not-so-pink dress. Boris and Jack tried to help her, though she assured them that she did not need their help, while straightening the ruffles on her dress, but she was very grateful for their attempts, though awkward at best.

The referee asked Lilly if she could still kick-a-berry, and if so they would resume play. She could, and they did. Jack patted Lilly on the back and gave her thumbs up. She might make a kick-a-berry player yet, he thought, though he was shocked that he had thought such a thing. Boris was very proud of Lilly, and thought she might have a permanent spot on their team, if she wanted one of course!

"Nice one, one to the face at that!" Boris chuckled. "I haven't even taken one to the face . . . you might have a shiner tomorrow. That was amazing Lilly, really amazing!"

Lilly got back in position and the kick-a-berry match resumed. Sander scored the first goal for Jack's team, with a header over Zeraz and Henri, who scored the second goal of the match tying up the game. Rosie was in goal when Jasper scored.

"Don't worry Rosie," Jack hollered, "that couldn't be helped – nice dive though!"

Lilly didn't take her eyes off the berry, not once. Jasper headed toward her, racing at a rate of speed she didn't know a fairy that wasn't in flight could actually obtain. She took a deep breath, stepped in front of Jasper, and kicked the berry as hard as she could. Jasper was stunned, as the berry flew into the air and landed at Boris's feet.

Boris ran with the kick-a-berry as fast as he could down the pitch. Jack waved his arms signaling he was open. Boris passed the berry to Jack. Jack dribbled up to the goal and he was about to take a shot when he noticed Pierre was in a better position. He passed the berry, and Pierre, who was ready, made the shot. It went in and they scored!

The referee blew his whistle; it was halftime. Both teams took a brief break, and water and pep talks were delivered. Everyone made a fuss over Lilly; she had truly taken one for the team! Her eye was starting to swell, but she still wanted to play. Rosie pointed at Lilly's dress. It was ruined, but Lilly didn't mind. She was certain that the wardrobe monitor would not be angry this one time, even insisting that if Jack could find pink kick-a-berry uniforms, well, she might just wear one. He assured her that he would take it into consideration, though he was doubtful Boris would look good in pink!

"Time to resume play," the referee announced and blew his whistle.

Both teams went back to the pitch, though this time they each went to the opposite side of where they had been playing. Sophie took off with the berry first. She passed it to Harold, who kicked the berry over Jasper's head, and then to Nadine who headed the berry into the goal . . . it hit the post – no point earned.

"Oh, that's terrible," whispered Lilly, but then realized it really wasn't. It was part of the match.

Boris managed to make the final goal, and it was a beauty. He dribbled past several opponents, in and out, in and out, and down the pitch. He passed the berry to Lilly, who got rid of it immediately by passing it to Rosie. Rosie passed to Jack, who took it a couple of strides and gave it back to Boris. Boris was glowing, as his legs moved faster than he thought possible. Just as he entered the goal zone, he passed to Jack, moved into a better position on the other side of Zeraz, and Jack passed the berry back to Boris. Boris kicked the berry as hard as he possibly could. It flew through the air over the goalies hands, though Henri dove for the berry, it was too high. It cleared Henri's fingertips and came down at just the right moment, securing the final goal of the game. Jack's team had won the kick-a-berry rematch!

The winning team was announced, hands were shaken, and compliments given and received. Boris and Jack grabbed Lilly, raised her up, and carried her on their shoulders.

"Oh dears, do be careful with little Lilly," Mademoiselle Francesca giggled, "I'm so proud of you dear," she said. "You played marvelously – you all did!"

Ivy jumped on the back of Pearle's chariot. "We did it Pearle and with Lilly, too, we did it – it was fantastic!"

Later that evening, while sipping hot lilac tea, Lilly couldn't help but smile. Her first real kick-a-berry match and they had won! Had she really taken one for the team? She looked at her red cheek and the place around her eye that was now slightly blue in the reflection of her teacup, *well may be I did*, *maybe I did*! Lilly thought.

"Hey this is for you," a familiar voice whispered, "it's a copy of *Fairy Gone Crazy*!" giggled Jack.

"Ah that's a great one!" said another familiar voice.

"What? Boris, you actually read it?" Jack giggled, as did Lilly, and, of course, Boris couldn't help but laugh with them.

"You know I'm kidding right, Boris? I know you read it . . . it's yours! I borrowed it for Lilly, and I was about to tell you!" said Jack with a grin. He handed Boris a great big fairy delight. "Here, this one's for you and this one's for you, Lilly. I asked Cook to make them."

They reminisced about the game, ate their fairy delights, and drank their tea; it had been an incredible day. Lilly knew that she would sleep well, as did Boris and Jack, since they were all tired, but Lilly couldn't help but wonder what else the mushroom patch possibly had in store for them!

About the Author

Amanda M. Thrasher, born in England, currently resides in Fort Worth, TX. Originally inspired to write a fairy story for her mother, she is now working on the third book in The Mischief Series, *A Spider Web Scramble in the Mushroom Patch.* Her other works include *The Ghost of Whispering Willow* and a Reader's Theater story for the Texas Municipal Court Education Center about teen driving safety, available for free at http://tmcec.com/DRSR/Readers_Theater.

For more information, visit www.amandamthrasher.com.

CPSIA information can be obtained
at www.ICGtesting.com
Printed in the USA
FSOW01n0725211116
27653FS

9 780988 856813